When I Dream of You

Genevieve Leanne Dominguez

Published by Genevieve Leanne Dominguez, 2024.

Also by Genevieve Leanne Dominguez

The Moonlight Thrills Series
Moonlight Thrills
Starlight Adventure
Evening Dangers
Midnight Perils
The Moonlight Thrills Series: The Complete Collection

Standalone
When I Dream of You
Phoenix: A Small Poetry Collection
Knight: A Small Poetry Collection
Meryle and Lancelot's Adventures

Watch for more at https://genevieveleanne.wixsite.com/ mysite.

To all the dreamers. You know who you are.

Chapter 1

July 1

I soften my smile, finally allowing my face muscles to relax. I've never liked talking about myself or hearing someone compliment me, but I'm grateful for the recognition. Sophie finishes her speech about my work and wraps her arm around me, beaming at the audience. The loud clapping and the clinking of champagne glasses dulls. A wave of sadness gently overtakes me. I swallow the lump in my throat, blinking away tears that I know are not my own.

When Sophie lets go, the sadness recedes until there is only a thin invisible tether and a haunting melody in the back of my mind, but I can ignore that. I involuntarily exhale a sharp breath of relief.

I smile, wave, and nod in gratitude to the crowd until Sophie gestures to the artist who's waiting. As she climbs the steps to the platform, I quickly leave the stage. Belle and Ren are waiting for me by the dessert table. Bruce is nowhere in sight. Belle has his leash handle on her wrist, so I follow the leash until it disappears underneath the dessert table. I scoff when I reach them and give my older sister a pointed look.

"What?" she says, her voice muffled as she finishes her chocolate cupcake.

"Where's Bruce?" I ask. Ren chuckles. Belle rolls her eyes and slips the handle off her wrist. When I gently tug the leash, the hem of the tablecloth moves and Bruce appears. There are crumbs around his mouth and his eyes are bright with excitement. He's wagging his tail so hard that his little butt shakes. He knows tonight is about him. Well, him and the pets of the other artists whose work is being showcased by Sophie.

As I brush the crumbs off his mouth, applause erupts throughout the art gallery.

"Oh, good! The speeches are over. Let's go check out your work!" Belle exclaims. Ren smiles at her enthusiasm and follows her lead.

The gallery is a long rectangular space that's been divided into octagonal shapes with plywood that's been painted soft white. Each artist's collection is housed in one of these funky spaces. The interior has been decorated based on the artist's medium and the theme of their collection.

"Whoa," I whisper as we pass by a collection of watercolors. Gold ribbons and silver wind chimes hang from the ceiling. The ribbons sway and the chimes softly ring. I look up and see two small fans situated opposite each other, blowing on the décor. A plaque on the left side of the entrance displays the name of the artist and their pet's name. The lettering underneath is smaller, so I can't read which animal shelter the proceeds are going to. I take a step closer.

"Layla, come on!" Belle says, waving me forward. Bruce happily obeys her command. I take a peek at the rest of the collections we pass by. Mine is the last one. I suppress a smile, remembering what Belle said when I first told her this. *"Oh, really? Why? Is it because she thinks pencil drawings won't sell as well? Oh, wait! That's not it. It's because she's saving the best for last."* I admit that a pencil drawing might sound a bit dull at first, but I've always liked the medium.

Belle and Ren gasp when we reach my collection. As they step inside, the neon lights overhead lazily swivel in their direction, coating them in hot pink, lavender, and electric blue hues. Sophie wasn't lying when she said my work didn't need much help to stand out. The neon lights are the only decor.

Before Bruce and I enter, I glance at the plaque: *Layla Dalì • Bruce Wade Dalì • All sales from the "Lunar Daydream" collection are final • 100% of the proceeds go to Paws & Smell the Chew Toys Animal Shelter.*

My drawings have been resized and printed on large canvases. I head to the first piece of my collection and study my strokes and blends, pleased with how defined and precise they still are. Belle and Ren admire each piece as if this is the first time they're seeing them. Bruce runs around the space, following the pace of the neon lights. I smile, grateful for the support and for how everything has turned out.

My primary career isn't art. I have a degree in business administration and work remotely as an Operations Assistant Manager (a fancy title for an administrative/human resources assistant) for an online education platform that teaches ESL to kids aged 3 and up.

I started drawing in high school, but I stopped in college. About two years ago, I got an idea for a drawing. I got off work that day, went to the nearest art store, bought some beginner sketching supplies, and began bringing my idea to life.

Finding a gallery that would showcase my work wasn't planned. Belle had suggested it, but I dismissed it because I didn't know where to begin and I hadn't started out with that intention. Three months ago, I was walking Bruce and decided to get him a doggy ice cream cup. The place I usually went to was closed for repairs, so I searched for the next closest ice cream shop. On our way there, we passed by a building that was under construction. A large pink sign was plastered on the glass door, calling for emerging artists who would like to support animal shelters. The next day, I called the number on the sign and spoke to the manager of the gallery, Sophie.

Several people enter my space, laughing and talking quietly. A man smiles at me and comments on how lovely my art is. A couple coos at Bruce as he runs past them to reach me. I pick him up and stroke his head, thanking the man who spoke to me while discreetly scooting to the exit at the same time. "Oh no, you don't," Belle says, appearing by my side in a flash.

"This isn't about you, remember? It's about where the money will go to, so sell every piece!" she whispers. She glances at Bruce. He's wriggling out of my arms and sticking his tongue out as far as he can to lick her arm. Belle wrinkles her nose and inches away.

"And take him with you," she adds.

I take a deep breath. Belle's right. I did this so that homeless animals could have a greater chance at finding a loving and forever home, just like Bruce did.

As I walk over to the couple that cooed at Bruce, I glance at Ren, who's talking enthusiastically with an elderly woman as if he's known her for years. How does he do it? He can strike up a conversation with anyone. Belle said that's one of the reasons why she fell in love with him. He's so friendly and kind. I've been told I have a kind face, but I'm too quiet and I've always had a hard time making friends.

Well, here's to hoping I can be an extrovert, at least for one night.

"Four out of ten pieces sold! That's a great start!" Belle says as we climb the stairs to the second floor of our apartment building.

"I agree. You were wonderful tonight, Layla. You should be proud of yourself," Ren says.

I smile, resisting the urge to yawn. Being social is exhausting. At least I didn't pick up anything from the people I interacted with. The sadness I sensed from Sophie eventually left.

Whenever she and I make physical contact, such as when I shook her hand when we first met or when she hugged me tonight, I sense sadness, but I don't know why. The only thing I'm sure of is that her sadness is not about me. And my rule is that if what I sense from someone does not pertain to me, then I leave it alone.

"Ooh, someone is moving in," Belle whispers.

At the end of the hall, three medium-sized cardboard boxes are stacked beside an open door. A loud *thump* echoes, as if someone is pushing something heavy up the stairs. Why are they moving in during the night? Belle must be thinking the same thing because she mutters to Ren, "What a great way to make friends with the neighbors by waking them up." She takes his keys from his hand and heads to their front door.

A tall, bulky man with his back toward us reaches the top of the stairs at the end of the hall. The back of his shirt is stained with sweat and he's heaving a bit. I can see now that he's hauling a sofa up. He takes the towel that's hanging out of his back jean pocket and wipes his face. A man's voice drifts up from below. "Everything okay?"

"Fine! Just give me a second. I didn't expect it to be so humid here," the man at the top of the stairs says. I nod, silently empathizing with him. Belle, Ren, and I are from Florida, so I'm used to the humidity, but that doesn't mean I like it.

The man turns around, as if he senses us watching him. He smiles politely and waves. Ren lifts his hand in response.

"Sorry about the noise," the man says.

"All good here," Ren replies. The man starts to speak when the man I couldn't see before comes into view. As he jogs toward us, he smiles a boyish, slightly sheepish smile.

My eyes widen and my heart flutters. I turn away for a second, self-conscious about my hair because I'm sure it's frizzy from the humidity. I'm also suddenly very aware that I still get shy whenever I see a gorgeous man.

"Hi, it's nice to meet you. I'm Noah and that's my friend, Theo. I apologize for the noise," he says, extending his hand to Ren. Theo's smile falters as he walks toward us. His expression ranges from shock to confusion, but it's directed entirely at Noah.

Noah and Ren shake hands as Ren introduces himself. "And this is my fiancée, Belle, and my soon-to-be sister-in-law, Layla," he adds, gesturing to Belle and me.

Bruce barks and Ren laughs. "Oh, that's right! I forgot about Bruce. He's the newest addition to our family. He's Layla's dog."

"He's handsome," Noah says, bending down to pet Bruce. I want to make conversation, but my words are stuck in my throat. All I can do is smile and hope my hair looks okay. Noah stands and extends his hand to me.

His skin is warm and his grip is firm. At first, I'm concerned about my handshake. I've never figured out how to do a proper one; I feel like my grip is either too tight or too lax. But my thoughts are abruptly interrupted by an image of a brick wall. A police siren rings in the distance. It's quickly replaced by a strange clicking sound. Bright lights flash across my mind, obscuring the brick wall.

I know what I'm seeing is about Noah, but I don't have time to fully process it because Theo's voice brings me back to reality. "I'm just here to help Noah move in, but I appreciate the warm welcome. I'm heading back to California tomorrow."

Belle's eyes light up. She was in love with California when we were teenagers. So much so that she wanted us to move there permanently. After she graduated high school, we visited Los Angeles, but the traffic alone was enough to make her rethink her plan to move. I was glad we didn't move and made no secret of it. I like the idea of West Coast beaches and sunsets, but the East Coast is my home.

"Is that where you're originally from?" Belle asks.

"Yes, this is the first time I've ever been across the country. It's beautiful here but very different," Noah says, flashing that same boyish, slightly sheepish smile. Does he know that his smile is gorgeous, especially when he pairs it with a bat of his eyelashes? After what I sensed from him, I don't know what to think. What I saw doesn't mean he's a bad person, but it doesn't mean that he's a good one either.

My ability has made me extremely cautious when it comes to socializing. I end up sensing random things from people, and I know I'll look crazy if I say, *"Hey, I had a vision that your friend is going to lie to your husband about you because she's jealous, so I'd start backing away from her if I were you"*.

But here's my dilemma: What if I see something awful and I could've prevented it by speaking up? This is why I keep my distance from people. Belle, Ren, and my co-workers are my only friends, though I'm not sure my co-workers consider me a friend since I don't socialize with them outside of work.

"What brings you here?" Ren asks. Noah's friendly expression freezes in place.

"Oh, it was just time for a change," he says, his voice upbeat but hesitant. Belle can hide her true feelings, but she can't hide them from me. The look in her eyes gives her away. She's nice to an extent – if someone pulls away, so does she. And she doesn't reach out again.

"Well, it was very nice to meet you both. Noah, I hope you'll like Georgia. Have a good evening!" She turns to face her and Ren's apartment, signaling that the conversation is over.

"Thank you," Noah says. A strange expression crosses his face. Theo glances at him with a sympathetic look and heads back to the stairs where the sofa is. *Noah's disappointed*, I think. But why is he?

This is one of those times I wish I could read minds, but my rule about minding my own business wins out in the end. I guess it doesn't matter so long as Noah means no harm.

The thought of a deep, peaceful sleep consumes me once I'm inside my apartment. I quickly change into my pajamas and crash into bed.

Chapter 2: Dream

I'm in a bedroom with walls that are covered in posters. I recognize some of them – Pretty in Pink with a red heart drawn around Andrew McCarthy's face, James Spader, Pat Benatar, and Bon Jovi. I'm sitting at the edge of a bed. On my left is a nightstand that holds a Rubik's cube, a pair of black fingerless gloves, and a light blue corded telephone.

Across from me is a dresser with a mirror. Clothes are scattered across the dresser top and a stack of textbooks teeters at the edge. Photos are taped to the mirror, but they're blurry. A desk is on my right. A boombox is in the center of the desk, and a song I vaguely recognize plays softly.

The bedroom door opens. Noah enters with two green glass bottles of Coke in his hand. Bruce is right behind him.

Noah sits beside me as Bruce lays down in a blue ruffled dog bed. Noah pops open the caps and hands me a bottle. There's a playful glint in his eyes as he takes a sip. When he's finished, he takes our bottles and places them on the nightstand. He caresses my hair then kisses me long and slow, gently biting my lower lip.

"I love you," he whispers. I giggle and press my lips together to keep the sensation of his lips on mine for a little bit longer.

"You're crazy. We haven't been together that long," I say. He sighs and falls onto the bed. That's when I notice what he's wearing – acid wash jeans and a black muscle shirt. I glance at my clothes. I have on the same jeans, but I'm wearing an off-the-shoulder purple top. Lime green, neon pink, and dandelion yellow bangles adorn my wrists.

Noah bolts up and wraps his arms around my waist. I squeal as we fall onto the mattress. He laughs and adjusts his body so that he's slightly on top of me. He kisses me passionately. Feverishly.

"Do you feel the same way?" he breathes.

I run my fingers through his hair. It's a medium brown color. When he tilts his head a certain way, the light reveals strands of amber and gold. His eyes are a beautiful shade of brown too – a blend of cognac and dark honey. His tanned skin, warm and smooth like satin, is flushed. When summer is over, I bet he's fair-skinned.

I trace his lips with my index finger. They're not full, but they're not thin either – they're the perfect shape to fit mine. But something's not right.

His facial piercings slowly pull me back to reality. I didn't feel the silver hoop on the left side of his bottom lip when we kissed. I try to touch the silver cuff on the upper part of his left ear, but I can't.

I realize Noah and I are not dating. I actually don't know him at all. But an invisible force is keeping me in place, compelling me to pay attention.

"I love you too," I whisper. He exhales a sigh of relief.

The phone rings. "That's probably my mom calling from work. She wants to make sure we're doing our homework," I say. Noah smiles, pecks me on the lips, and sits up.

I pick up the phone, but it's not my mom. It's my ex-boyfriend. He wants to know if we can meet up tonight to work on our project.

We were grouped together with two other people in our Algebra II class yesterday. The project counts for 25% of our grade. It's due in two weeks.

"No, I can't tonight. I'm sorry. What about tomorrow?" I glance at Noah.

"Who is it?" he mouths. I cover the mouthpiece with my hand and tell him, but I don't hear the name. Noah rolls his eyes.

"I'm sorry, but this is for our math project. It counts for a chunk of our grade," I say.

Noah laughs dryly. "I doubt he's worried about his grade that much."

I grimace and lift my hand off the mouthpiece. "I can meet up tomorrow," I say.

After we agree to meet at the library, he tries to make conversation, but I gently cut him off.

"Yes, Noah's here. Oh. Okay. Yes, I will. Okay, bye," I say. After I hang up, I turn my attention to Noah.

"He says 'Hi.'" Noah raises his eyebrows.

"He didn't say it in a rude way," I mutter. Guilt overtakes me for a moment. My ex really is a nice guy. Then I remember why we broke up.

One day, we got into an argument over what his father really thought of me. That night, he went out and kissed one of his friends. The next day at school, one of her friends told me what had happened. When I confronted him about it, he didn't deny it, but he didn't fully admit it either. I could tell he was sorry, though. I tried to forgive him and forget about it, but I couldn't.

Plus, there was the matter of our social standing: He's rich and I'm not.

Although I can't recall her name or face, I know the girl he kissed is pretty and – most importantly – rich like him. I'm sure his father would approve of her immediately.

"You shouldn't feel guilty over his mistake," Noah says.

"You're right," I say, but I still feel bad. None of this would've happened if I had listened to my mom when she said to never date above our social status.

"I have an idea," Noah says. He walks over to my boombox and turns up the volume. I recognize the song – "Never Gonna Give You Up" by Rick Astley.

Noah smiles and holds out his hands. "Let's dance!" he says.

I laugh at his silly moves. Bruce barks and jumps out of his bed to join us. I'm having so much fun that I don't register the noise on the floor at first.

When I feel my feet pushing something around, I stop and look down. I gasp at the gleaming jewels. Rubies, sapphires, opals, emeralds, and pearls are strewn on the ground, and they're multiplying fast. I'm already up to my ankles in them.

The edges of my vision blur. Noah's laughter and Bruce's barking fades. I look up and see myself in the dresser mirror.

My hair is voluminous and fanned away from my face in a feathery fashion. I have on lavender eyeshadow and bright blue eyeliner. A rosy blush covers my cheeks and my lipstick is bright pink.

Voices a few feet away from me grab my attention. A guy and a girl are leaning against the wall near the door. They look to be about 17 or 18. The girl is holding a dog, a pug with a pink collar, in her arms. She turns to me and somehow, I know her name.

"Hey! Do you understand what I mean?" Melody asks.

I gasp when I wake up. It takes me a few seconds to remember where I am and what year it is. I run to the bathroom and strip off my sweaty clothes, shivering all the while. I change into a sweatshirt and sweatpants and splash some water on my face, hoping that will snap me out of the coldness that's enveloping me.

I glance in the mirror. I'm back to me – straight, layered dark brown hair that's a little past my shoulder and *not* full of freeze hairspray and dark brown eyes that are free of colorful makeup. My skin color stands out to me. It puzzles me until I remember why.

In my dream, my skin and hair were lighter. Belle and I are half-Puerto Rican and half-Hawaiian, but we're often mistaken for being just one or the other. Belle has curly hair and a curvy body, so people think she's full Puerto Rican. I'm slim and have medium tan skin and almond-shaped eyes, so people guess that I'm Hawaiian or Asian.

In my dream, I resembled Melody, who was fair-skinned and had blonde hair. The guy she was talking to didn't look like Noah. He was dark-skinned, but he and Noah were dressed exactly alike, just like Melody and I were.

Chapter 3

One of the great things about living across from Belle and Ren is that I can go over for breakfast anytime. Ren had to go work early today, which means I can tell Belle about my dream. I haven't told Ren about my ability, and I don't think I ever will. Aside from our parents, Belle is the only one who knows and – most importantly – believes me.

I've mentioned what I can do, but I'd like to explain it a bit more thoroughly. Ever since I was a girl, I've been able to sense things from people. It mostly comes to me in my dreams, but, from time to time, I'll see things while I'm awake.

I'll see something play out in my head as if I'm watching a movie. Other times (which is most of the time) I'll get flashes in my mind of colors or images or I'll hear songs. Sometimes, I can discern what someone is feeling, such as when I knew Noah was disappointed last night. I can also dream from another person's perspective, though it's hard to figure out when that has happened.

My mom believes psychics and mediums exist, but I don't fall into those categories. I can't communicate directly with the dead nor do I always have clear visions. When I was little, my mom did extensive research until she found a name for my ability: I'm a Sensitive Soul. Both my mom and dad taught me how to analyze what comes to me, but I can't always figure it out.

At first, I wanted to help people. I considered a career in law enforcement after I graduated high school, but I decided against it. How would I explain to my boss that I was able to solve a case if there wasn't sufficient evidence? What if a criminal got away because there wasn't sufficient evidence, but I knew they were guilty? I wouldn't be able to let it go; I'd become obsessed with catching them.

"I would stick to what you've been doing and leave it alone," Belle says as she sets a slice of blueberry bread on my plate. I take a bite, slowly chewing and trying not to replay the dream in my mind.

"I mean, it's been working out great for you so far, right? Besides, none of it makes sense. You and Noah dating in the 80s? He doesn't look old enough to have been born then, but he could look young for his age. I doubt it, though. Maybe it was his good looks that made your brain mushy" Belle says, waggling her eyebrows. I giggle. When it comes to men, Belle is always on the lookout for me.

"Thanks anyway for listening," I say, finishing my slice.

"Anytime," she says with a smile. After I help her with the dishes, she snaps her fingers and gasps.

"Ooh, I almost forgot! Come by my store after work today. I have a surprise for you."

I narrow my eyes, suspicious of her excitement. Some of my sister's "surprises" are really favors she asks of me. One time, she asked me to model a line of evening gowns and I immediately agreed. I momentarily forgot I don't like the spotlight. It was fun because it was for Belle, but it wasn't me at all. There were too many hair extensions, makeup that felt like heavy cream on my face, and endless flashing lights.

"Sure," I say slowly. She scoffs.

"Honestly, Layla, if I had as much talent as you, I would flaunt it. Oh, wait! I'm already doing that," she says, a triumphant smile spreading across her face. I roll my eyes and quickly leave before she can continue to criticize my introverted personality.

Belle and I are not alike. I used to wish I was more like her – ambitious and tough with a witty comeback for anyone who tried to tear her down. But no matter how hard I tried, I couldn't be like her. It took me a while, but I've learned to love who I am – a mellow, quiet dreamer.

I arrive home a half hour before work starts. Bruce is still asleep, but I like to fill his food bowl and change his water before he wakes up. I adopted him a couple months ago and quickly found out he's a night owl and *always* hungry. After he graduated puppy training class, the trainer sternly advised me that I should break him out of these habits, but I like his quirks too much. If he was a cartoon character, he'd be a regular dog by day and a secret agent by night.

I tidy up my room a bit then turn on my work equipment. That doesn't take long, so I'm left with fifteen minutes to spare. On impulse, I grab the notebook I keep in my desk drawer for to-do lists and drawing ideas and write down the dream. I'm so absorbed in making sure I have the details correct that my alarm to start work startles me when it rings.

A company-wide meeting is being held first thing this morning to introduce Avery. One of our best artists recently left, so we've been shorthanded in that department, but that changes today. Everyone gives Avery a warm welcome, and even though he already met her in the final interview, her manager looks like he wants to cry out of relief.

As Avery introduces herself, I smile and stay attentive, even though I've already heard this before. She lives in California and has just graduated with a master's in digital arts. When she didn't get promoted at her previous company, she decided to look elsewhere.

My eyes drift to her flaming red hair. It's pretty, but it's so bright that I can't help but think it's not her natural color. As she adjusts her glasses, I study the shape of them. She's wearing oversized round frames that remind me of a style that was popular in the 80s. It emphasizes her big bright blue eyes. Avery seems nice, but there's something about her. I haven't been able to think of the right way to explain it until now.

She looks too dreamy, as if she could easily be whisked away to a fantasy land. I cringe inwardly, realizing I have no room to talk, but I remind myself that I'm thinking from an HR standpoint. In other words, I hope she's a good employee and lasts, at least through the production of our newest education program.

After work, I head to Belle's store. I considered taking Bruce, but I checked the weather before I left and decided against it. Stormy, humid weather agitates him.

I don't like to drive too much and thankfully, Belle's store isn't far from where we live, so I decide to walk, not caring what it means for my hair because I'm headed back home afterwards.

Belle is a fashion designer and businesswoman. She opened her first boutique here in Atlanta, and she's currently working on opening a store in New York. She designs clothes for women of all sizes. What makes her fashion unique is that she never follows what's in season. She specializes in "vintage" wear.

Belle's new boutique will open early next year, and I can't wait. I love fashion, but I'm not good at it, so I'm thankful she likes to dress me, especially for when we visit New York.

When I enter, she squeals and rushes to my side, thrusting her arms upward. "Look, look!" she exclaims.

One of my drawings is displayed on the wall above the checkout counter. "Thanks, sis," I say, beaming as I give her a hug.

"Only five more pieces to sell," she sings. I pull back and give her a look and she smirks.

"I'm closing up in a few minutes. Ren is coming home late tonight. If you want, we can grab takeout from that Chinese place you like," she says.

"Thanks, but I want to get back to Bruce. He doesn't like storms," I reply. She huffs as she starts to straighten some clothing racks.

"You baby him too much," she says. I give her the same kind of smirk she gave me, and she sticks out her tongue. It's not that Belle doesn't like Bruce. He just made a bad first impression when I introduced them. He peed on the floor of her store and she screamed so loud that one of her customers whirled around, lost her footing, and fell. Bruce was so excited by the commotion that he ran to the lady that fell and licked her face.

I apologized to Belle's customer and explained that I had adopted him that day. He was so happy to be out of the shelter and I didn't think about taking him to potty beforehand. Thankfully, she didn't mind. Belle, however, has not gotten over it. It didn't help that I pointed out her customer fell because she screamed. To this day, she maintains it was Bruce's fault.

After hearing my stomach grumble for the second time, I regret not taking my sister up on her offer. I trudge up the stairs to my apartment.

Lightning flashes and thunder booms overhead. I jump and glance at the sky. The clouds are dark and stirring. The scent of rain is so strong and crisp that it momentarily dries out my nose. I sneeze loudly and pick up my pace.

When I reach the top of the stairs, the hallway is empty and silent. A gust of hot wind sweeps through. I'm not alone.

Am I being watched? Targeted? I grip my key as if it's a weapon and inch forward, debating on what the smarter move is. Should I run to my apartment and lock myself in with Bruce or run to my car, lock the doors, and call Belle? No! I can't leave Bruce by himself.

"Hi, Layla," a familiar voice says. I turn around and see Noah climbing the stairs, wearing a friendly but hesitant expression. Bright white lights flash in rapid succession, obscuring him. I hear the same clicking sound I heard when I shook hands with him. A dark outline of a person appears in my mind. Their face is hidden behind an object I can't make out.

"Hi," I say, hoping I don't sound scared. I tuck my hair behind my ears, wondering if it's as frizzy as it feels.

"How are you?" he asks.

"Okay. And you?"

He shrugs. "It's going. Doing as good as I can be."

I bet this is what the brick wall I saw when we first met signifies – he either doesn't know how to open up or he prefers not to. If he prefers not to, then it doesn't make sense why he's attempting to make conversation. I figure it must be my first guess – he doesn't know how to open up.

It's amazing how many details I absorbed about him last night. Up close, he looks exactly as he did in my dream. I wasn't exaggerating his looks either. He's beautiful. I even remembered his height correctly. He's a couple inches taller than me (around 5'10" or 5'11"). He has a nice body too – slim but defined.

"Work's not going so great?" I ask.

"No, it's not that. It's just... stuff. Sorry, I don't mean to be so evasive," he says, flashing me a sheepish grin. Red colors his cheeks.

"It's fine. Take care," I say, quickly turning on my heel because I really don't want to continue the conversation if he's going to make it difficult for me. Some people are so hard to figure out, and I'm starting to think Noah could give me a headache.

Later that evening, I think of the obvious: What if Noah was planning on harming me and I sensed it? Instead, the tension left my body when I saw him, as if I subconsciously knew that I was safe. As if I knew that being near him was the right choice.

Chapter 4: Dream

"Bruce!" I scream.

My throat is raw and aching. I reach the end of the park trail, deflated and on the verge of tears. I slump down and sit on the edge of the sidewalk. I tremble as I struggle to catch my breath. There are so many other places to look, but I don't know where to begin.

"Layla?"

The light of a lamppost a few feet away shines down on a male figure walking toward me. I recognize that voice. It's my ex-boyfriend. I know his name now – Brandon. I groan quietly and stand, regretting that I didn't ask Noah to come with me tonight.

When Brandon reaches me, I notice something in his hand. It's a flyer. "MISSING" is at the top of the page in bold red letters. Below that is a picture of Bruce and my contact information.

But this doesn't feel real. Bruce isn't missing. Or is he? My mind fogs up and I'm sucked back into the dream.

It's been four days since Bruce disappeared. Images of him being locked up in a pound or alone and shivering in a sewer tunnel race through my mind. I cover my mouth to try to hide the sob that escapes from me. How did this happen? Bruce is supposed to come with me to college then to vet school. How can I even think about becoming a veterinarian if I can't protect him?

Brandon gazes at me in pity. "I saw your flyer today and I wanted to see how you were doing. I called your house and your sister told me you were here," he says.

"That's very nice of you, Brandon, but I'll be okay. Bruce will return soon," I say. He smiles sadly. He knows I don't believe what I'm saying. He steps forward with his arms outstretched as if to hug me. I take a step back and he freezes.

"I'm sorry, but I don't think that's appropriate because –"

"I understand," he says, but there's a catch in his voice. "Can I give you a ride home?"

I shake my head. "Thank you, but I'll be fine. I saw a payphone not too far from here. I'll call my sister and have her pick me up."

Brandon sighs. "Please, Layla. It's going to get dark soon. I'm sure Noah will understand."

I glance at the sky. The sun is setting fast. My mom and sister will be mad if I don't come home soon. They know how worried I am about Bruce, but I know they would remind me that nothing good will happen if I deliberately put myself in danger.

"Okay," I say. Brandon smiles and leads me to his truck.

Once we're inside, he places the flyer on his lap and grabs a case of cassettes from the backseat.

"Would it be okay if I put on some music?" he asks. I nod and he pops in a tape. He turns down the volume and starts driving.

After a few minutes, he says, "I saw it's been four days since Bruce went missing. I'm guessing you haven't had any luck?"

"None" I reply quietly.

"What if I could help with that?"

I glance at him. "What are you talking about?" I ask.

"I could offer a reward to whoever finds him. I'm thinking... $5,000?"

My eyes bug out. "$5,000? You would do that?"

It would take years to pay Brandon back, but getting Bruce back would be worth it.

"Of course, Layla," he says, looking at me with a tender expression. My stomach sinks when I realize I can't take him up on his offer. What if he wants something other than money in return? That's when I remember something important – something he told me right before we broke up.

"How are you going to get the money? You said your dad froze your credit cards. Does this mean his business is doing good again?" I ask.

"Don't worry about that. I've got it covered. What do you say?" he says.

Before I can say yes, a dog barks behind us. I jump and turn around. Melody is in the backseat, holding a pug with a pink collar. She smiles at the dog and strokes her head. A guy is beside them. I've seen him before, but I can't remember where. He's looking out the window with a serene expression on his face.

I shift in my seat to get a better look at him, but I stop when something in my jeans pocket pricks my leg. I reach inside my pocket. Small, cold objects poke my palm. I grab a handful and take them out.

When I open my hand, tiny diamonds reflect the fading sunlight. I don't have time to think about how or where I got them because my pockets are bulging now. I try to grab more, but they're multiplying and spilling out of my pockets and onto the seat.

"Hey!" Melody calls out. I look up and see her staring at me with an expectant expression, either unaware of or uninterested in the jewels.

"Do you understand what I mean?" she asks.

I gasp as I bolt up in bed. My entire body is ice-cold, as if I've been sleeping in a freezer. This time, I don't bother to change into warmer clothes because I know what I'm feeling isn't real. It's a result of the dream.

I grab the notebook I wrote my first dream in and scribble out this one. When I finish writing, I realize the guy I saw in the backseat beside Melody is the same guy from my first dream – the one who was dressed like Noah. I also know that the jewels are extremely important, but I don't know how or in what way.

Chapter 5

September 21

The dreams have stopped. I'm relieved, but I'm also a bit concerned. It feels like they didn't completely leave – just that they've been put on hold. I haven't said anything about it to Belle because what if I'm exaggerating? Sometimes, I think it's the constant rain that's making me edgy. I love cloudy weather, but this feels different.

Sophie called me yesterday and asked if I could come to the gallery for a meeting today, so Bruce and I are on our way there now. We're both wearing raincoats and I have my umbrella, but I think we'll be home before the real rain begins. It usually just drizzles during the day.

I'm a little giddy because I think Sophie is going to ask me to be in her winter show. All my pieces from my first collection have sold, and the animal shelter the proceeds went to sent me a thank-you basket for the contribution. If I'm right about what Sophie wants to discuss, I can't wait to tell Belle and Ren the good news.

As we near the corner of the sidewalk, Bruce freezes and the hair on the back of his neck stands up. When I hear him growling softly, I realize it's too quiet. The streets are empty of people and cars. All the businesses around us are closed. There's a white paper taped to every door, but I can't read it from where I'm standing.

Sophie's art gallery is in an area of Atlanta that can double as the upscale side of New York. In other words, we're in a place where the average cost of buying an outfit is $1,000. I was so distracted by my meeting with Sophie that I wasn't keeping an eye on my surroundings. Even though we're on the good side of the city, I've watched too many crime shows to know bad things can happen anywhere, anytime.

I pick up Bruce, but before I can take another step, chaos erupts. Glass shattering. Shouting. A high-pitched alarm ringing.

A good distance away is a black van parked in front of a jewelry store. Several men dressed in black and wearing ski masks come around the corner of the van. One of them flings the back doors open. The van jiggles a bit as all but two climb in. The men who didn't get in slam the doors shut. One of them looks to his left and right then nods at the other. They take off their masks. The man who's facing me disappears around the passenger side of the van while the one whose back is toward me starts walking to the driver's side. He takes a set of keys out of his pocket.

Every time I watch a crime show, the person who doesn't get out of harm's way irritates me. If I'm really invested in an episode, I'll yell at them to move, run, or hide. Don't just stand there and be a witness. That's exactly what I do.

I stand there, unable to move or think, when the man looks my way. He stops and does a double take. It's Noah.

He tilts his head toward the van and shouts something, throws the keys through the open window on the driver's side, and starts running in my direction. I scream and take off, realizing a second too late that he might have a gun. I zigzag, hoping that'll throw off his aim if he shoots at me.

I'm not sure if I should continue running straight, so I round the next corner I see and find myself in a narrow alley. For a second, I'm surprised it's so clean until I remember where I am. A hysterical laugh bubbles up in my throat. Of all places to be running from a criminal, it had to be on the good side of the city. And it had to be someone I know. If I don't lose Noah soon, Bruce and I might end up dead.

Bruce barks and tries to wriggle out of my arms, but I'm holding him so tight that I know he's not going anywhere. I'm at the end of the alley when I hear Noah.

"Layla, stop!"

I gasp and spin around to face him. His mouth is set in a hard line and he's holding a gun in his right hand. Bruce's barking fades, as if he's realizing the gravity of the situation.

The last time I saw Noah was the day I cut him off because he was starting to annoy me. I should've been nicer to him, although I don't think that will make him think twice about harming me now.

A few drops of rain land on my face. I don't try to wipe them away for fear of giving Bruce too much wiggle room. Noah holds up his hands, as if to show me he means no harm, and slowly walks toward me.

Is this what my dreams were trying to tell me? That I was going to witness Noah robbing a jewelry store?

"I'm not going to hurt you, Layla," he says, his voice careful. He extends his right arm to the sky, aiming the gun in the same direction.

"When you hear the first shot, I need you to lie down," he says.

I should run. But he's closer now. Just a few feet away.

"Now," he says. The gunshot rings in my ears. I lie down. The cement is cold and damp.

After he fires another shot, Noah quickly closes the distance between us.

He kneels by my head and places his lips so close to my ear that I feel his lips moving against my skin as he whispers. It sends a tingle through me.

"When I leave, count to 60 then go home. Do not call the police. I will come by later tonight and explain everything. Do you understand?" he asks.

Tires screech to a halt near us. He jumps up. It must be the van. I close my eyes and tilt my head to the side.

"Ready?" a man calls out.

"Yeah, we're good!" Noah says.

"Are they dead?"

"Like I said, we're good. I know someone who will clean this up. I'll call them once we get out of here."

I hear Noah jog away. The van door opens and closes. When I'm sure Bruce and I are alone, I open my eyes and count to 60. Then I get up, shaking, and run.

Chapter 6

I still don't understand why I listened to Noah. It can't be because of his looks. I'm not *that* shallow. Unless I am. I shake my head and let the steam of my tea warm my face for a moment before taking a sip.

I did what Noah asked me to do because I didn't want to die. Maybe I should call the police now...

What if he's planning on killing me tonight? No, I don't think he is.

I clutch my phone, resisting the urge to call Belle and tell her everything. I don't want to get her involved. But what if she finds out somehow? She'll be so upset that I didn't go to her for help.

Then there's Sophie. She called while I was in the shower and left a voicemail, asking if I'm okay because she heard what happened and wanted to know if I was in the area during that time. She sounded anxious, but I haven't mustered up the courage to call her back. What if I say something I'm not supposed to?

I groan and rub my temples. My mind feels like a huge pile of gray goop. I finish my tea, set it on the end table beside the sofa, and glance at the clock. It's 11 o'clock sharp. Is Noah still coming?

Bruce runs over to me, stands on his hind legs, and places his front paws on the edge of the sofa. He has a cheerful expression, and he's wagging his tail softly. He wants to play.

When we arrived home, he jumped out of my arms, ran to his food bowl, and gobbled down everything. I checked him for bruises, but he seemed fine. A silly thought breaks through all my serious ones and I smile. What if he really is a secret agent by night? It would explain why he doesn't seem emotionally spent from what happened earlier today.

A knock on the front door makes me jump. Bruce runs to the door and sniffs at the bottom. I get up slowly and tiptoe over. When I glance through the peephole, my stomach flip-flops. Would it be naïve of me to open the door? I don't give myself time to think about it.

Noah has changed clothes. He's wearing a brown leather jacket that matches the color of his eyes and a black V-neck shirt. He enters and stands in the entryway, his arms crossed tight over his chest. He studies me silently, brows furrowed in concentration as his eyes roam over my face. It's unnerving yet attractive. I feel like he's trying to read my mind. What if he can? Heat creeps into my cheeks.

"I think we should sit," he says.

Those are his first words? An apology for chasing me down the street with a gun or "*Thank you for not going to the police*" would be nice. It might even help break the ice a bit. I picture a giant glacier between us and press my lips together so I won't laugh hysterically.

As we sit across from each other at my dining table, Bruce sits beside him and looks up, his tongue hanging out of his mouth. It looks like he's smiling. Does he know something that I don't? Noah smiles at him then glances at me.

"May I?" he asks, reaching for Bruce as if to pet him. I nod and he strokes his head. Bruce gets up after a few seconds and heads to my bedroom.

"He's a smart one," Noah says.

"Yes," I reply. It's like he knows we want privacy and he's giving it to us. Noah sighs and begins to study me again. After a few seconds, he flexes his hands and clears his throat.

"I know I said I would explain everything, but I'd like to begin with you, Layla. Where were you headed today?"

A small fire flares up in me. It's rare for me to feel this way. I've never liked confrontation. I used to avoid it, even if it meant taking the blame for something that wasn't entirely my fault. It had to be something extremely bad for me to speak up. And even then, I didn't speak up much.

It wasn't until after I graduated college that I grew out of it. When I started my career, I realized I had made it to "real life" – working, paying bills, taking care of myself, etc. And I can't let anyone walk all over me anymore.

"Why are you asking me that? You should be glad I haven't called the police yet. I thought you were going to kill me," I snap.

Noah blinks, clearly surprised. I don't blame him for that. Belle has always told me that I look too nice.

"Why were you robbing a jewelry store? *That's* the most important question," I add. Noah leans forward, props his elbow on the table, and covers his nose and mouth with his hand. His eyes stand out this way, and I notice they're wide and kind. *Puppy eyes*, I think.

I don't realize we've been staring at each other, silently studying one another, until he removes his hand from his mouth and speaks softly. "Layla, I am the police. I'm undercover."

I'm relieved that I don't find jewel thieves attractive.

"Oh! Well, that answers the most important question," I reply. He laughs but abruptly stops, shaking his head as if he's remembering he shouldn't do that. A twinge of disappointment runs through me. I understand why he wants to keep this professional, but I don't think I'd mind getting to know him on a personal level.

"You play your part well. I would never guess you're an officer. Your piercings look real," I say.

"Detective," Noah says, correcting me, "And my piercings are real. The men I'm trying to take down identify their specialty by their piercings. It's a code." He leans back in his seat and folds his arms across his chest.

"But I've already said too much. I can't share any more information. I need to know everything you saw, starting with why you were in the area today." He takes a pen and a small notepad out of his jacket pocket. As he's doing this, I think of something and I narrow my eyes. What if he's a really good liar?

"Where's your badge?" I ask. Without hesitation, he reaches into his pants pocket and takes out what looks to be a black leather wallet at first glance. When he flips it open, his badge gleams in the light. I lean forward and inspect it. I don't know what I'm looking for, but it looks real enough. When I look at him, the corners of his mouth are turned up slightly, as if he wants to smile.

"You're not supposed to be carrying any credentials when you're undercover," I say, proud of myself for remembering that from a cop show. He smiles.

"I brought it in case you asked to see it," he says. I'm not sure I believe him yet, so I say the next thing that pops in my mind.

"You look young to be a detective," I say.

"I'm 30," he replies as he opens his notepad and clicks his pen. "How old are you? 21?" he asks.

"I'm 28," I say.

He nods, but his eyes are on the notepad so I can't try to figure out what he's thinking. He takes advantage of the beat of silence.

"Let's start at the beginning. Where were you headed today?" he asks.

I tell him everything – why I was in the area, what I saw, and how I felt. He interrupts me at times, asking for minute details that I didn't think I could remember until he made me consciously think about it.

He asks what I do for a living, how often I go out, and what places I frequent. Then he gives me instructions on how to lay low. It makes me a bit nervous until I realize the man who was driving the van thinks that Noah killed Bruce and me.

It's after midnight when we finish. He rips out the page he's written his instructions on and hands them to me. Then he sets his notepad on the table and looks at me with a sympathetic expression. My breath catches in my throat.

"I'm sorry for scaring you, Layla, but I had to make it look real. Thank you for not going to the police."

I can't stop myself from glancing at his lip ring. What does it symbolize? He said he couldn't share any more information, so there's no point in asking him.

"Thank you," I murmur. He smiles and stands. Bruce runs out of my bedroom and heads toward him. Noah laughs at his enthusiasm and kneels down to pet him.

"Can I tell my sister about this? She won't say anything," I say.

He grimaces. "The less people that know I'm undercover, the better."

I groan as I stand up. I don't want to lie to Belle. Correction: I can't lie to Belle. She'll figure out something's up. An idea comes to mind. Noah never said "No". That's my loophole.

"How long do I have to follow these instructions?" I ask, holding up the piece of paper he gave me and gently waving it.

"It shouldn't be much longer."

Well, that was helpful. It occurs to me that he knows more about me than I know about him. I know he had to ask, but I'm not used to sharing so much information about myself. It makes me feel exposed. Vulnerable. I'm usually the one who knows more about someone.

"Fine," I say, brushing past him as I head to the door, not bothering to hide my irritation. He places his hand on my forearm. His touch is light, but I *feel* it and my irritation disappears.

His touch is electric, but it's not the kind that zaps me and makes me tingly. It's like I'm near a cozy fire that's making me feel alive. The fire emanates a sweet, intoxicating scent. The flames whisper to me that I won't get burned. I take a step closer to Noah. Just one taste of his skin and I'll know what euphoria feels like.

"Noah is my real name," he murmurs. The fog that was clogging my mind fades away. I blink rapidly, as if I'm waking up from a dream. A really good dream.

Noah is looking at me with an expression I don't understand. He removes his hand from my arm and inches away from me.

"What do you mean?" I ask.

"My undercover name is Eli. Noah is my real name," he says. I remember the way his friend, Theo, reacted the night we met.

"Is Theo a detective too?" I ask. He tilts his head in confusion.

"Yes," he replies slowly.

"Is that why he looked shocked when you told us your name? He knows you're undercover?" Noah's expression relaxes.

"Oh, yes," he says, chuckling, "He got on me about that, but I told him it'd be okay."

"Why did you tell us? You had no reason to," I say. He thinks about it for a moment.

"I just felt that I could," he replies. I don't press him about it because I get it. Sometimes, you just get a sense about someone. I'm glad he knows we're good people – me, my sister, and Ren.

Lightning flashes, briefly shining through my closed window blinds, and thunder booms overhead. Bruce whimpers and scampers over to me. I scoop him up and stroke his head.

"He doesn't like storms," Noah observes.

"Not at all. But he'll be okay," I reply.

Noah smiles and playfully winks at him then opens the door. He looks back at me and his expression softens.

"Thank you again, Layla. I'm sorry you had to go through this."

I don't respond because I'm reeling from his winking. I'm glad it wasn't directed at me because I'd have probably fainted from attraction. I don't know if that's a thing, but even if it isn't, I'd have definitely been the first to suffer from it.

Chapter 7: Dream

"You still haven't told me how you got the money," I whisper.

Brandon remains focused on his textbook. I close mine a little too forcefully. The librarian makes a frustrated sound. She places her index finger on her lips and glares at me. I mouth "Sorry" and quickly turn away to stifle my laughter. Her oversized round glasses and puffy bangs make her angry expression look comical. Brandon coughs to hide his laughter and closes his book.

"I didn't think you'd be so interested in how I got Bruce back,"
he says. His eyes drift to my lips. Guilt pinches the center of my chest, but I ignore it. He hasn't told me how he wants me to pay him back, and it's making me anxious. Plus, I doubt his father gave him $5,000 without wanting to know the reason why.

My mom and sister thanked Brandon when he returned Bruce to me last weekend, but I saw the strained look in their eyes. After Brandon left, they scolded me for allowing him to help me. I knew they were right, but I was desperate to get Bruce back. I called Noah that night to tell him what happened, but he didn't answer. He hasn't returned any of my calls for the past week, and he hasn't been in school either.

I've been thinking about going by his house after school today to check on him. The look Brandon is giving me right now is the deciding factor. I'm leading him on and it's wrong.

Finding out how I'm going to repay Brandon back isn't important. Noah needs to know what I've done. I hope he doesn't break up with me.

I stand up and begin putting my books in my backpack.

"Is everything okay?" Brandon asks.

"I'm sorry, but I have to go," I say.

"But we just started studying," he whines.

"Noah hasn't been in school this week, and I want to check on him," I reply. He nods, but I notice the slight twitch in his jaw.

"Can we study tomorrow?" he asks. I hesitate to answer. How much can I refuse him?

"I'll tell you how I got the money," he adds in a playful tone. Dread erupts in the center of my chest and slithers to the tips of my fingers and toes. This is why my mom and sister were so mad. When will I stop owing Brandon?

"Sure," I finally say.

He smiles wide. For a moment, I remember the way I used to feel about him. What made me think he and I could work out? Even if I were to get a high-paying executive job after college, his family still wouldn't accept me. Besides, it doesn't matter anymore. I belong with Noah. I'm in love with him.

It's strange to realize this while I'm talking to my ex-boyfriend in our school library. I wish Noah was here right now so I could tell him. But I wouldn't want to stay with him if he had accepted help from his ex-girlfriend, who had made it obvious that she wanted him back. What have I done?

That's when I notice Brandon's watch is missing.

"Hey, what happened to your watch?" I ask. He glances at his bare wrist.

"Oh, it needed a new battery. I dropped it off yesterday, and I'm going to pick it up today. I feel strange without it," he says. I know he's lying because he's not looking me in the eye. That's exactly what he did when I confronted him about the girl he kissed.

I'm in an ice cream parlor, sitting across from Noah in a booth. He moves his spoon through the mushy liquid that was once chocolate ice cream. After a few seconds, he pushes the cup away and looks out the window that's on our right. Bruce is lying on the floor beside us, cheerfully licking his ice cream, unaware of the tragic situation I've just learned about.

I notice someone in the background – a person covered in blood red paint. I can't tell if it's a man or a woman. They're sitting several booths away from us, sipping a milkshake. I start to slide to the end of my seat because I want to find out who this person is, but something invisible pushes me back. My mind becomes hazy. I try to resist it, but it's strong. The same invisible force that's keeping me in place gently turns my head to the right and tilts my chin up. The haze in my mind disappears.

The moon is full tonight. I can see it clearly through the window that's beside Noah and me, but the fluorescent lights overhead drown out any light the moon may have thrown our way and casts a shadow on Noah's face.

Noah's dad is the manager of a local jewelry store. Last Friday, his store was robbed and he was shot. He's currently in a coma. The doctors don't think he's going to make it.

Noah was the one who found him. He hasn't left his side until a few hours ago when his mom made him go home and get some rest. What makes everything worse is that his father wasn't supposed to be at the store at the time it was robbed.

I don't know what to say or do that will ease Noah's pain. The last thing he needs to hear about is my situation with Brandon. What if the doctors are right and his dad dies? I should've checked on him sooner. Instead, I was worrying about how I was going to pay Brandon back.

Noah leans forward and props his elbows on the table. "There's something you should know. Something I haven't told anyone else about," he says. He reaches in his jeans pocket.

When he places the watch on the table, the expensive-looking gold gleams. I don't have to inspect it to know who it belongs to.

It doesn't make sense. Brandon's rich. Why would he be involved in a robbery? My stomach sinks and fear clenches my heart until my chest hurts. Is this how Brandon got the money to pay for Bruce's return?

"He did this," Noah whispers, balling his hands into a fist.

"He did this," Noah mutters again through gritted teeth. I swallow the hard lump that has formed in my throat. I have no choice. I have to tell him this is my fault.

A tap on the window startles me. I should scream at what I see, but I know this dark and faceless figure that's waving at me. Noah must recognize him too because he scowls and snatches the watch off the table.

"Let's get out of here," he says.

When we exit the parlor, the dark figure is waiting for us. His hands are clasped in front of him, and his head is inclined forward, as if to indicate submission and kindness – that we shouldn't be frightened. Noah stiffens and grabs my hand. The dark figure steps forward.

When he speaks, his voice is distorted. I strain my ears to try to understand what he's saying, but I only catch a few words – "father", "apologies", "watch", and "deal".

Noah is enraged. He shouts at the man and gently pulls me closer to him. I pick up Bruce and we start to walk away. I glance back and although this man is faceless, I know he's upset. A tremor runs through me. I tell Noah to walk faster.

My mom and sister have always told me to be careful. Noah and I shouldn't have walked here. Why didn't we take his car?

Bruce starts to bark. Noah turns back. His eyes widen at what he sees behind me. He yells at me to run.

We run past a few stores before Noah turns down an alley. I tell him we need to stay on the main street, but he insists this is a shortcut to the police station. We're almost at the end of the alley when the man appears. I scream and stop. Noah steps in front of me, blocking me from him.

He yells at the man. Silence follows. Noah turns around to face me, his eyes full of fear. He grabs my hand and tells me to run. Tears fill my eyes and spill over as I tell him no. I won't do it. I won't leave him.

A strange, loud sound occurs. It makes my ears ring. Noah flinches as if someone has hit him from behind. He collapses to the ground. I scream and fall to my knees beside him.

The man approaches us. He's holding a gun in his hand. As he comes closer, I look at him and plead with him to help, but I know he's not going to. He meant to shoot Noah.

A hole, darker than the rest of his face, appears where his mouth should be.

"This is your fault," he says, his voice still somewhat distorted. He aims the gun at me and something pinches my chest hard. I look down and see blood streaming out of a hole in my chest.

I try to stand, but my knees buckle and I drop to the ground beside Noah. Bruce's barking turns into low whimpers. He walks over to me, sniffs my cheek, and lies down beside me. The man picks him up. Bruce starts growling, and he tells him to shut up.

I want to yell at him to leave Bruce alone, but it's getting harder to breathe. My chest is cold. I watch the man walk away, his steps quick and silent.

I glance at Noah, who's gazing at me with a sorrowful expression. He starts to speak, but I shake my head. I don't want him to lose his breath like I'm losing mine. Besides, I know what he's going to say. He doesn't have to apologize. This is all my fault.

My legs feel like blocks of ice. I can't move. I can't speak. But I still feel. Noah's hand grips mine. His palm is cold. He whispers that everything's going to be okay. He tells me he loves me.

I close my eyes, wishing I could tell him about my part in this. I didn't want this to happen. I just wanted Bruce back.

When I open my eyes, I see that Noah has fallen asleep. Does this mean... No, he can't be. He just can't be. He just needs to rest. Someone will find us and help us. I guess I should get some rest too. I'm sure someone will wake us once we're in the hospital.

When I close my eyes, something hits my face. I open my eyes to hundreds of small jewels – diamonds, rubies, pearls, amethysts, and more – hurtling toward me. I try to scream and move, but I can't. I shut my eyes tight as they pelt my face.

Soon, I'm buried in them. Hopelessness gnaws at me and hot tears slide down my face. How will anyone know I'm here if I can't scream?

The jewels clink and clatter and begin to move. Someone grabs my hand and pulls me up. I gasp for air, swatting at my face so the stinging sensation will go away.

"Hey!" a familiar voice says.

Melody is sitting beside me, staring at me with an exasperated expression. A guy I feel like I've seen before is on her left and a pug with a pink collar is on her right.

"Do you understand now?" she asks.

I jolt up, my heart beating so fast that it feels like I've just gotten off a rollercoaster. I jump out of bed and call for Bruce. He comes running, tongue hanging out of his mouth and tail wagging. I pick him up, climb back into bed, and hold him for a while. When I start to calm down, a song begins to play in my head. I hum the melody as I release Bruce and head to my desk. I write down the dream. I don't realize I'm crying until a teardrop lands on the paper, staining it.

I understand now why I've been so cold when I wake up from these dreams. I've been dreaming from Melody's perspective and Noah has been playing the part of her boyfriend. Brandon murdered them.

Chapter 8

October 4

I never thought I would be anxious to leave my apartment.

I know I shouldn't be complaining about being alive and safe, but it's knowing I can't leave that gets to me. Noah didn't give me his number and I forgot to ask for it, so I can't call him. Even though he's just a few doors down from me, it feels inappropriate to barge in on him. What if I blow his cover?

At first, staying home was productive. I cleaned every nook and cranny. I caught up on laundry, gave myself a pedicure, and watched some movies I had been wanting to see for a while. Belle and Ren did my grocery shopping. To show my appreciation, I cooked dinner for them and made enough so that they would have leftovers during the week.

The rain finally stopped and autumn is now in full swing. I opened my living room windows a couple days ago, and someone must've been cooking with their windows open because a delicious blend of cinnamon and nutmeg wafted in. I envisioned a slice of pumpkin bread and a salted caramel latte from my favorite coffee shop. That's when the restlessness hit me. When would I be able to go out?

It's affected Bruce too. He's been whining and scratching the front door at the times I usually take him for a walk. I haven't asked Belle or Ren to take him out because I don't want to risk him being seen.

I haven't had any more dreams about Melody, and I don't think I will. I have a feeling that what she showed me is linked to the jewelry store robbery I witnessed, but I don't know how to find out more without looking strange or suspicious.

I stopped Belle from knocking down Noah's door the day after he came over. As I suspected (and braced for), she was furious about what happened. She's always masked her fear with anger, which means I had to calm her down for hours, explaining to her over and over what happened and what Noah said to do. She wanted to know the exact security measures he was taking to keep me safe, but I stopped her from talking to him by assuring her that I would go to him if I hadn't heard from him in the next two weeks, which means I have to talk to him tomorrow.

My alarm to start work rings. I sigh and face my computer, forcing myself to have a pleasant expression for today's meeting.

Avery and I are the first ones to arrive. After we exchange small talk, she asks how my art is going. I'm surprised she remembers that detail about me because I mentioned it in passing when I interviewed her. She giggles and flutters her hand at the screen.

"I remember all kinds of details about everyone! I believe knowing the small things about someone is what makes an artist great. The better I know someone, the better I can capture their emotions and thoughts and make others believe they know them too."

"I agree! It's the small things that round out a person. And to answer your question, it's going great. I've been asked to participate in the winter show for the art gallery that displayed my previous collection," I say. Avery's eyes light up and she claps her hands.

"How exciting! Speaking of collections, can I show you the characters I've been working on?"

As she goes through each character, she tells me their name, their primary color palette, and their main personality traits. All of them are interesting and add to the program we're developing in one way or another. The last character is an outline of a male figure.

"Have you named him yet?" I ask. She places her hand over her heart.

"Yes, but I don't want to say right now. He's very dear to me because I'm modeling him after my boyfriend," she says.

"That's sweet. How long have you been together?" I ask.

"Two years, but we're on a break," she replies. Uh-oh. A break in a relationship doesn't sound good, but what do I know? I haven't dated in a while. My last boyfriend lied to me about giving a girl a ride home from work. I didn't have enough proof to confront him, but I knew he was lying. And if he could lie about that, what else could he lie (or had he already lied) about? It didn't hurt much when I broke up with him, so I took it as a sign that he was not the right guy for me.

"I'm sorry to hear that. I hope you'll work things out soon," I say.

She smiles and adjusts her glasses. "Thank you, but it has nothing to do with our relationship. He needs some space right now, and I completely understand why. Once things have settled down for him, maybe he could pop in and say hi to the team!"

I hope I don't look like I feel sorry for her when I smile. Avery seems like a nice person. A little too whimsical but nice.

Later that day

Bruce chases after his toy, barking excitedly as he skids across the living room floor. I'm rolling out dough for a pie crust and trying to come up with ideas for a winter collection at the same time.

Autumn leaves scattered around a bonfire. A lamppost shining down on a couple kissing in Paris during wintertime. A rainy night in the city. Sunrise over a meadow covered in snow and pockmarked with wolf paw prints.

Thinking about art reminds me of when I returned Sophie's call, which was right after I talked to Belle. She was so relieved and urged me to be safe. It was a bit strange how insistent she was, but I think it has something to do with the sadness I've felt from her. She might've gone through something traumatic or someone she loved did.

A knock on the door interrupts my thoughts. It's probably Belle coming to remind me about talking to Noah tomorrow. Just to be safe, I ask who it is before opening the door.

"It's me, Noah."

My heart picks up speed. I wipe my hands on a dish towel, shushing Bruce who's still barking excitedly because it's not helping my nerves.

When I open the door, Noah smiles and glances over me. "Cooking?" he asks.

I brush some flour off my jeans. "Baking, actually. Pumpkin pie," I say.

"That's one of my favorites," he says, grinning. I blush, wondering if I'll ever get over how beautiful his smile is.

"May I come in?" he asks and holds up a folder. I tell him to sit wherever he likes. I offer him something to eat or drink, but he declines and heads to the sofa. Bruce runs to him and places his front paws on the edge of the seat cushion he's sitting on and rests his head on his knee. Noah chuckles and pets him.

I sit down beside him, unsure if I should ask what's inside the folder.

"How have you been doing?" he asks.

"Getting a bit anxious," I admit with a shrug, "Do you know how much longer it'll be until I can go out?"

He sighs and runs his hand over his face then musses his hair. "I'm sorry to ask this of you, Layla, but could you please give me one more week?"

"Ugh, I guess."

He gives me a sympathetic smile. "I'm sorry. I should be thanking you," I mutter.

He shakes his head. "No, it's okay. I actually came here to ask you for a favor. I should've done this sooner, but would you mind taking a look at these photos and see if you can identify any of these men?"

He opens the folder, takes out some mug shots, and spreads them on my coffee table. I only recognize one – the man who took off his mask during the robbery.

"Will I have to testify in court?" I ask. Noah hesitates.

"I hope it doesn't come to that," he says.

I'm not sure how I feel about his answer, so I focus on the mug shots. I look carefully at each photo because I don't want him to think I'm hurriedly picking one. The song I heard when I woke up from the dream about Melody and her boyfriend's murder drifts into my mind. It's been doing that these past two weeks. It'll come into my mind then fade away after a couple minutes. When I completely forget about it, it comes back again. I researched the song, but the only thing I found out was that it was released in the 80s, which wasn't a surprise.

"What are you humming?" Noah asks. I glance at him, a bit startled by his tone of voice. I didn't realize I was humming. He's looking at me with the same discerning expression he had the first time he was here.

"Nothing," I stammer, realizing a second too late that's the wrong answer. Noah's eyes narrow.

"Is that the name of the song?" he asks.

"No," I reply quietly. I wish he didn't have the ability to make me nervous. First, I was nervous because of my attraction to him. Now it's because he's looking at me like I've committed a crime.

"So what is it?" he asks.

"What is what?" I say.

"The song, Layla," he says, his voice stern and commanding.

"It's not a crime to hum a song," I reply, biting my lip when the words leave my mouth. What is wrong with me? Why can't

I answer his question? I snatch the mug shot of the man I recognize off the table. Maybe I can redirect the conversation back to his initial question.

"That's him. That's Jake," I say, handing the photo to him. He doesn't take it. Instead, he sets his mouth in a hard line and stands. What did I do now?

"How do you know his name?" he asks, crossing his arms over his chest.

Uh-oh. My cheeks flare up. I don't know how to get out of this. I glance at the mug shot, hoping Jake's name will be on it somewhere. Noah's expression softens and he sits back down. He takes the photo from my hand and sets it on the table.

"Has someone threatened you?" he asks.

"N-no," I stammer. He inches closer.

"You can tell me," he whispers. His breath, warm and sweet, sweeps across my face. Drowsiness engulfs me. It's like I'm lying on a bed of velvety clouds, watching stars collide across Noah's face. I've never smoked or drank or done drugs, but I think one taste of his lips will be my own personal high. I place my hand on his shoulder, gently pulling him toward me.

"Layla, please," Noah breathes. I blink rapidly as I'm pulled out of my stupor. His eyes are wide, his gaze shifting from my eyes to my lips, but he doesn't pull away.

"I'm so sorry," I exclaim, springing to my feet. I shove all the mug shots back into the folder, and I thrust it at him. Then I race to the door and open it wide. I suck in a mouthful of cold air, but it doesn't cool the fire in my face.

Noah walks toward me with a dazed expression. He opens his mouth, but I cut him off.

"The song is 'Right Here Waiting' by Richard Marx. I don't know how I knew Jake's name. No, I'm not being threatened. Now if you don't mind, I prefer to be alone," I say, pushing him out the door before he can respond. After I lock the door, I slide to the floor and bring my knees to my chest.

I just tried to kiss a gorgeous man. No, a gorgeous detective. I groan and softly bang my forehead against my knees a few times. What happens now?

Chapter 9

October 11

"I still can't believe you tried to kiss him!" Belle says, laughing. I wish I had never told her what happened between Noah and me. She hasn't stopped teasing me about it since. I hope I never see Noah again, though I think that's highly unlikely.

Ren chuckles quietly as he grabs a chip and dips it in our salsa bowl. He hasn't commented on what I now deem as "My Most Embarrassing Moment Ever", and I appreciate that. It's one of the many ways he and my sister complement each other. As Belle waves down our waiter so she can order more salsa for us, I sit back in my chair, allowing the crisp evening air to wash away my thoughts of Noah.

We're at a rooftop restaurant that overlooks the city. Belle and Ren invited me out to dinner tonight. I think they feel bad that I've been cooped up in my apartment for three weeks, but I won't question a free meal. The restaurant doesn't allow pets, so I took Bruce for a walk before I left. He was just as ecstatic as I was to get some fresh air.

I contemplated asking Noah for permission to go but quickly decided against it. I did ask Belle for advice, though.

She thinks everything has blown over and my "death" has been forgotten. I hope she's right.

The rooftop is enclosed by a railing that goes up to my waist when I stand. My chair is right against the railing, so I lean over a bit, admiring the golden haze of the city lights.

There's something mesmerizing about the city at night. It's as if everything is connected yet distinct from each other. I trace the path of a street with my eyes, gazing at the people rushing or ambling to their destination. Then I follow a unique pattern of lit windows on a skyscraper, wondering what kind of work is so important in there that's causing so many people to work late.

Here in Atlanta a forest is woven throughout the city. The trees are as alive as we are, thriving among concrete, brick, and steel. Some trees are evergreen while others are shedding their leaves for the year, blanketing the ground in scarlet, gold, and burnt orange hues. The height of the trees is breathtaking, but when the city lights cast a glow on them, it enhances their mysterious aura.

"So Halloween is in three weeks," Belle says. Ren and I glance at each other and smile because we know what that means.

This time of year is rush hour for Belle. She gets so many sales and receives so many requests that it's been tough for her to keep up. She's finally put more employees on her payroll, and Ren is one of those people. He's going to manage her finances. It won't become official until she opens her new boutique, but he's slowly starting to take over now.

"So you're both going to be super busy and can't be bothered," I say. She beams.

"You know me so well, baby sis."

I roll my eyes and Ren laughs. "Are you going to dress up this year?" I ask.

"We haven't really thought about it," Ren says, looking at Belle for confirmation. She shakes her head.

"I don't think so, but if you have something in mind, let us know."

I wrinkle my nose. I don't like going out on Halloween. When we were kids, Belle and I went to a party. I was a pumpkin and she was a princess. Somehow, we got separated and a boy wearing a werewolf mask sprang out from behind a large bale of straw and scared me. I slipped and fell into a tub of water that was meant for apple bobbing. I cried all the way home because I thought my pumpkin costume was ruined.

When the waiter brings our food and another round of chips and salsa, a band of musicians emerges from behind the curtain at the area that's set up for live entertainment. When they begin playing, I squeal. "You didn't tell me it was jazz night!" I exclaim.

Ren chuckles. "We wanted to surprise you."

"We hope everything works out soon," Belle adds. Pity flickers across her face. In spite of her teasing, she's worried about me.

The noise in the restaurant has reduced to hushed voices and gentle clinking of glasses and plates. A twinkling melody tickles my ears. The pianist is entranced by his own music. His eyes are closed and his body sways as he plays. As the music builds to a crescendo, the rest of the band follows his lead, their fingers expertly moving up and down their instruments. The drummer bobs his head and steadily taps his right foot, glancing around the restaurant as he plays. It's as if he knows the song by heart, and he makes me believe that I know it too. If I reach into the farthest corners of my mind, I can remember where I've heard the song before. Perhaps when I was completely innocent – unaware of the filthy, violent parts of the world and unafraid of the people who mask their darkness with kind words and generous actions.

Is this how Melody viewed the world? She was so young. How could Brandon be so cruel as to murder her and her boyfriend and steal her dog? Unless he's not the killer. Maybe I jumped to conclusions too soon.

Applause throughout the restaurant startles me and jerks me out of my thoughts. The pianist announces they'll be back in 15 minutes and steps off the stage. The rest of the band follows him.

I check my watch and am about to ask Belle how long she and Ren plan on staying when a bright flash of light blinds me. A police siren rings in the distance. A series of rapid *clicks* follows. A street and a murky figure appear. The figure is holding a rectangular object against their face. Light emanates from the object in brief bright flashes.

A man with blurry features appears. It looks like he's walking away from the murky figure. I realize the person holding the object is following the man. I think they're taking pictures of him. Oh, I get it now. The object they're holding must be a camera. Even though I can't see the man's face, I think I recognize him. It looks like –

"Hi," a familiar voice says. Everything I was seeing disappears. My heart drops and my stomach flip-flops. I wince as I turn around.

Noah shouldn't be this beautiful. He's wearing a black blazer over a white button down shirt and black slacks. Several of the buttons on his shirt are undone, revealing his smooth chest. His face is slightly flushed and his piercings glint in the soft lighting.

I want to run and hide where he won't be able to find me. Why is he here? Has he been keeping tabs on me?

It's rare to see Belle at a loss for words. Her eyes are wide as she glances between Noah and me. Ren saves us from responding. He stands and offers his hand to him. They exchange a bit of small talk before Noah glances my way.

"I apologize for interrupting your evening, but I was hoping to speak to Layla alone," he says.

"Why, *detective*?" Belle asks. She gets up and stands next to Ren. She seems to have recovered from her initial shock.

She angles her body so that she and Ren block Noah from me. A few people glance our way but quickly return to their conversations. Noah clears his throat and looks at her steadily.

"I assure you I'm doing everything I can to keep Layla safe –" he says, stopping when Belle holds up her hand.

"I didn't ask what you're doing to keep my sister safe. I asked why you want to speak to her right now. We're busy," she says.

"Belle, it's fine," I interject. I stand and walk around her and Ren. I knew I was going to have to talk to Noah eventually, so I prefer to get it over with now.

"Are you sure?" she asks, keeping her eyes on Noah.

"Yes," I answer.

"Fine. We'll wait for you over there," she says, nodding at an empty table.

"I can take Layla home," Noah offers. She looks at him up and down.

"As long as you don't chase her down an alley with a gun again," she says. Ren's polite expression freezes in place. Noah raises his brows and straightens his stance.

"I assure you I will never do that again," he says, his voice calm but firm.

Belle doesn't respond. She nods at Ren instead who slowly takes his wallet out of his pants pocket. They head to the front of the restaurant. When they're out of sight, Noah sighs and relaxes his posture.

"Your sister is intimidating," he says. For a moment, I forget what happened between us and I want to ask why he couldn't be stern with her like he was with me. Before I can, he asks, "Do you want to take a walk?"

"Sure," I say, hoping it doesn't sound as forced as it feels.

We walk in silence for a while. I start to relax, letting the bustling nightlife around us ease my tension.

"I didn't find you by coincidence. I followed you to make sure you were safe, but I'm sure you figured that out," Noah says.

"You're not mad?" I ask. The look in his eyes is soft and warm, but there's something underneath – a determination.

"I'm just as concerned for your safety as your sister is. It's dangerous to put yourself out here right now, Layla. You don't know who knows who. I made your death believable, but I can't be 100% certain. The men I'm working with act like they trust me, but they don't know the meaning of trust. Do you understand what I mean?" he asks.

His question reminds me of Melody's – *Do you understand now?*

"I think I do," I reply quietly.

"I'm so close to setting up a meeting with their boss. It shouldn't be much longer," he says.

The words come out before I can think them through. "Yeah, I know. You said that three weeks ago."

He smiles and his serious expression morphs into an amused one. Why do I get the feeling that's exactly what he wanted me to say?

"That's true," he agrees. A beat of silence follows.

Does he want me to ask? If it's a trap, I don't care. I'm curious.

"So what's different now?"

He steps in front of me, still smiling playfully. He's so close that I have to back up a bit. I don't want to embarrass myself in public by trying to kiss him again. What is it about him that makes me so disoriented?

"If I tell you a bit about myself, will you answer one question?" he asks.

"Depends on the question," I reply. He continues to smile as if he knows something I don't. His confidence is alluring.

"I'll take those odds," he says. He starts walking again and begins to explain how he became a police officer.

Noah entered the police academy when he was 21. He always wanted to be a cop, but he honored his mom's wish and went to college after high school. College didn't work out for him, so his mom gave him her blessing to enter the academy. He was a patrol officer for four years before he applied to become a detective.

He quickly became known for his ability to influence others. Whether it was victims, suspects, or his fellow officers, he could empathize with people in a way that got them to open up. His chief describes it as a "rare charisma". If I ever meet his chief, I'd tell him he was spot-on and that I have also fallen victim to Noah's charms.

A few months before Noah turned 30, his chief approached him with an offer to go undercover. One of the chief's friends lives in Atlanta and needed help with a case. He didn't want to risk one of his officers going undercover since most of them have either been raised here or have lived here for years, so he asked Noah's chief if he knew anyone who would be up for the job.

"I needed a change of scenery, so I accepted," Noah says.

The case he's working involves a series of "sporadic" jewelry store and art museum robberies that have been occurring for a year and a half throughout the U.S. Noah has infiltrated the group of thieves who are responsible for the heists. He's been obtaining evidence to build a case against them.

The robberies are considered sporadic because no heist has been performed the same way. It was hard to locate the thieves until the police found a posting on the dark web a few months ago. They were looking for someone who could shut down a large amount of surveillance technology and electricity for a day without being tracked.

Behind the scenes, the police shut down all the cameras in the area where the robbery was going to take place. They also turned off the electricity for all the businesses on that block and sent an email to the owners and supervisors of each business, pretending to be the companies they use for internet and light. It was explained as an unforeseen malfunction and that all businesses would have to remain closed for the day.

After Noah showed proof that he had done this, the thieves blocked off the vehicle entrance to the area the night before the robbery, masking it as construction work. It's not common for undercover officers to break the law, but Noah was approved to partake in criminal activity because he had to gain their trust.

"Seeing you shocked me, but I had to act fast. After you explained to me why you were in the area, I checked and discovered that the art gallery didn't shut down that day. No one could explain how that had happened. I couldn't figure it out until...," he trails off.

Something about the robbery bugs me, but I can't ask him about it without looking strange. I remember hearing an alarm, people shouting, and glass shattering. Noah described the crime as silent.

"Until what?" I ask. He stops walking and gives me a pointed look.

"I don't believe in coincidences. It wasn't by accident that you were in the area that day. I know you are not connected to these crimes in any way. I'm sure of this because I ran a thorough search on you and have been keeping tabs on you for the past week.

"You shouldn't have known Jake's name. The song you were humming the last time we talked is very important, though I don't think you know that. Also, why did you do what I asked you to do the day of the robbery? How could you trust me after I had chased you down with a gun? I'm not arrogant. I don't believe I can influence everyone I meet."

Noah crosses his arms and furrows his brows. "Which brings me to my question for you: What can you do?"

It can't be. He can't know. People don't really believe. "What?" I stammer.

He takes a step closer. "What can you do?" he asks.

I use the phrase everyone uses when they know exactly what the other person is talking about. It's a weak countermove, but I have to try.

"I don't know what you're talking about," I say. Noah doesn't back down.

"Yes, you do," he says quietly.

What's the right thing to do? Keep denying it or admit the truth?

"I understand if no one has believed you before," he says, reaching for my hand.

"Leave me alone," I snap, yanking my hand out of his reach. His serious expression dissolves into a plea.

"Please, Layla. You have a gift from God."

My irritation vanishes. That's what my parents told me when I was little. *You have a gift from God, sweetie.* It suddenly shames me to think that I've been wasting His gift my whole life. But how can I help if no one believes?

"Only my parents and sister know. I've never told anyone else," I reply softly.

"I believe you," he says, beaming. His eyes roam over my face. It's not the kind of inspection I expected to endure if anyone ever found out about what I can do. He's looking at me like I'm special. Like I'm someone to be adored. My eyes narrow.

"You want something," I say flatly. Of course he does. He's only interested in me because I can help him.

Noah's cheeks redden. "Well, that's not the only reason why I believe you. I –"

I whirl around and start walking away.

"Layla, wait!"

But I don't wait for him. He proved to be what I expected. If someone knows about my gift (and actually believes me), they'll eventually want something.

Chapter 10

I hate when I'm wrong and it eats away at me until I make things right. Or, at least, try to. After I got home last night, I realized I was right about there being a connection between my dreams and Noah's case. I want to do everything I can to help Melody and her boyfriend's spirit rest in peace, which means I need to apologize to Noah.

When I knock on his door, there's no answer. I strain my ears to hear if there's any movement inside. After a few seconds, I knock again. The door opens slowly. Noah blinks, clearly shocked.

"Hi," he says.

"I'm sorry," I say. He gives me a bewildered look.

"For what?" he asks.

"I was rude last night and I assumed that you wanted my help in your personal life, but you need help with the case, right?" I ask. He smiles and opens the door wide.

"I'm the one who overstepped, but I'm glad you're here," he says, motioning me to come in.

His apartment is exactly like mine, except he doesn't have as much furniture or décor. A picture of (who I assume) are his parents and younger brother sits on top of a bookshelf. Next to the bookshelf is a small desk. Stacks of paper and manila folders are piled high on it.

A freshly heated frozen dinner is on top of a TV tray that's situated in front of his sofa. Across from his sofa is a flat screen TV where a movie plays on low volume.

The color palette of his apartment – dark gray, light blue, and white – is pretty but gives me a twinge of depression. I can't help but think that this is a really comfortable hiding space. But that makes sense because he's undercover.

"Sit wherever you like. Would you like something to drink?" he asks as he walks to the fridge.

"No, thank you," I reply. I head to the sofa and sit at the edge. I've always felt strange in other people's homes. One wrong touch and I could end up sensing something I shouldn't know.

Noah sits close to me, though not close enough for us to touch, and waits patiently. I'm grateful for that. How do I begin to explain what I can do? I feel like I shouldn't tell him anything. If I'm being honest with myself, I don't want to tell him. Excluding my parents and Belle, I've kept this part of myself secret for so long that it's hard to take down the wall I've built.

That's when it dawns on me. Noah has been hesitant to open up too. I remember the brick wall I saw when we shook hands and the way he acted before I witnessed the robbery. Now he's reaching out, readily believing me. It would be nice to have a friend who knows who I truly am.

So I don't think about how to tell him; I just do. He interjects at times with a question or two, but he mostly listens. I emphasize that what I sense is not clear most of the time and

I cannot communicate directly with the deceased. I've learned to decipher what comes to me, but some things still don't make sense. For example, I could dream about a lamp, but it's actually about a phone.

When he doesn't have any more questions, I tell him about my dreams, but I don't tell him that he and I played the role of Melody and her boyfriend. I don't want to make things awkward between us, especially now that I've opened up to him.

"I've written everything down. I can show you tomorrow," I offer. He nods, his eyes fixed on the floor.

"You said the girl's name is Melody, but you don't know her boyfriend's name?" he asks.

"No, I don't. I'm sorry," I say. He shakes his head.

"No, don't be. I'm just working something out in my head. What did you say her ex-boyfriend's name was?"

"Brandon," I say.

"And she had a sister?"

I nod. "But I don't know her name."

He gets up from the sofa and walks over to his desk. After sifting through a few papers, he finds what he's looking for – a yellow sticky note.

"Sophie manages the art gallery that your works were displayed in, right?" he asks.

"Yes, she asked me to do a collection for her winter show," I say. He smiles.

"I'd like to see your work sometime."

I picture myself drawing Noah's body and blush. "Sure," I mumble. *Keep it together*, I tell myself. *He's the only friend you've got and you don't want to mess it up.*

"Would you mind coming with me to visit Sophie tomorrow?" he asks.

"Oh! Sure, but, um, didn't you say last night that I need to be more careful?"

Noah smiles again, but it's the kind that makes my heartbeat quicken. Heat races through my body and my toes become tingly. It crosses my mind that he's doing this on purpose, but I immediately squash the thought. The only reason he's opened up to me and kept tabs on me is because I was a witness to the robbery.

"You're safe with me," he says, his voice a bit husky. Or am I imagining that tone?

"Why do you want to talk to Sophie? Do you think she's involved in the crimes?" I ask. But I don't need him to answer. As soon as the words leave my mouth, I realize she's involved – but not in the way one would initially think.

Sophie's gallery is empty of art right now. A couple of cushioned benches, upholstered chairs, and small mahogany tables are scattered throughout the well-lit space. Classical piano music plays softly from the speakers overhead.

"Layla, how good to see you!" Sophie says, her heels clacking loudly on the floor as she runs toward me. She embraces me and gives me a quick, affectionate squeeze.

I don't know why I didn't think of it sooner. Sophie has never told me her exact age, but I'd guess she's in her early sixties. I mentally smooth out the lines on her forehead and the creases near the corners of her eyes. She has light – almost white – blonde hair and blue eyes, and she even has the same nose as her.

She's Melody's sister.

"And who do I have the pleasure of meeting? Your boyfriend?" she asks. I stammer out an objection, though I'm pretty sure anyone who's paying close attention to me would guess that I'm attracted to Noah. Fortunately, he offers her his hand, calm and graceful.

"It's nice to meet you, ma'am. I'm Detective Everett. Layla is my friend."

She glances between us then gazes at his lip ring for a second too long. Noah must notice it too because he takes out his badge. She tenses.

"Is everything okay?" she asks, her voice low and full of worry. He smiles politely and bats his eyelashes. Her eyes widen a bit. I'm glad I'm not the only one affected by Noah's good looks and charisma.

I wonder if he's purposefully used his charisma on the women he's dated. Does he have a girlfriend back in California? He seems like the type of man who would mention it... but maybe not. Now that I think about it, he might go back to California after he's completed the case. It's possible he wanted a change of scenery because he went through a bad breakup. He never did tell me the exact reason why he decided to go undercover.

"Is there somewhere we could sit and talk?" Noah asks. Sophie clasps her hands together and looks around, exhaling shakily. Is she thinking of Melody?

After a few seconds, she says, "Follow me."

Her office is in the back of the gallery. It's filled with art, mostly paintings and drawings, but there are some sculptures on her massive bookshelves. The floor is carpeted, but it's not the industrial kind. It's a cream color and plushy. Her desk is large and made of glass. I can see everything in her drawers – pens, receipts, keys, candy, and folders. A picture frame is beside her computer. I want to see if it's Melody, but she asks us to sit and takes her seat behind the desk.

"Do you remember the robbery that took place about three weeks ago?" Noah asks.

"Yes, that was the day I asked Layla to come here so we could discuss a collection for my winter show." She beams at me.

"Layla is very talented," she adds. Noah smiles softly and rests his hand on top of mine. The gesture startles me. The warmth of his hand is quickly replaced by a strong *zap!*

I feel like a steel pole that's been struck hard by another steel pole. My ears are ringing and my insides coil in excitement. If Noah and I were alone, I wouldn't be able to stop myself from grabbing him and smashing my lips against his.

Sophie's eyes flicker to our hands and sadness clouds her face. Is she remembering Melody and her boyfriend?

I stuff my free hand in my pocket and dig my nails into my palm so that I can remain focused on the conversation.

"I agree. Layla is very special. Did she tell you she witnessed the robbery?" Noah asks. Sophie's eyes widen and her mouth opens in shock.

"What? No, I didn't know that!"

She turns to me. "Please forgive me, Layla. I didn't know –"

Noah interjects softly. "It's okay. I know you weren't aware of what was happening. I'm here to inform you that the robbery is connected to your sister's murder."

Sophie blinks rapidly, as if she's waking up. "What?" she breathes.

"Your sister, Melody, was murdered in 1989 along with her boyfriend, Jackson," he says.

After a moment, she whispers, "Yes".

"I looked into your sister's murder. Jackson's father's killer was found and apprehended, but he didn't confess to killing Jackson or your sister. There wasn't enough evidence to tie him to the murders either. To this day, it has remained a cold case."

Noah leans forward, staring intensely at Sophie. She mimics his movement, her eyes locked on him.

"I think I know who killed your sister," he says.

Chapter 11

October 29

When Noah ran a search and kept tabs on me to see if I was involved in the crimes, he looked into Sophie too. That's how he found out about Melody and Jackson's murder. When I told him about my dreams, he connected their unsolved case with his current one.

As to who murdered Melody and Jackson, Noah said it's a 50/50 guess. I know he suspects Brandon, but I don't know who else he suspects. He won't tell me his theory. He said he wants my reaction to be genuine if he's right.

On the day we visited Sophie, he explained to her why he suspects Brandon. She admitted that she suspected him too, but she dismissed it when he offered to help get her business running.

Melody was 18 when she was murdered and Sophie was 22. Sophie had been in college then, double majoring in art history and business. She had drafted a plan to start her own art gallery and had been trying to get a loan from the bank, but her request had been continuously denied.

Two years after Melody's death, Brandon offered to invest in Sophie's gallery. He refused to receive any of the profits. His only request was that 100% of the proceeds from one showcase would go to animal shelters as a way to honor Melody. Sophie readily agreed because Melody loved animals. She wanted to become a veterinarian.

Sophie showed us a picture of Melody holding a pug with a pink collar – the same dog that was in my dreams. Her name was Luna. I wasn't surprised by what she said next because of what I had already seen in my dream: Luna went missing and was never found.

"I do believe that Brandon loved her, but he was never going to leave his family. It's one of the reasons why I encouraged her to be with Jackson," Sophie said as she wiped tears from her eyes.

"Melody met Jackson at their school's homecoming dance, but she was still with Brandon at the time. I remember she came home and told me the song that was playing when they met. It was by Richard Marx, but I don't remember the name of the song."

"She said, 'Sophie, isn't it strange? It feels like a moment I'll never forget.' That's when I knew that she and Brandon weren't going to last much longer. She was meant to be with Jackson," Sophie said, smiling sadly.

Noah revealed to Sophie that he's undercover and explained a few things about the case he's working on. He had been trying to secure an invitation to meet the leader of the heists, who he's now certain is Brandon, but he didn't want to risk exposing himself, especially now that he had spoken with Sophie.

"This is where I would like your help, if you are willing," Noah said to me.

Brandon's wife, Melissa, is hosting a costume party the day before Halloween, which is tomorrow. The party is for their friends and potential investors of Brandon's business, which means the thieves are not invited. The chances of Noah's identity being exposed at the party are slim to none.

Sophie has secured a party invitation for Noah and me. We will pose as husband and wife, the owners of a successful veterinarian franchise in Canada, who are looking to invest in a thriving American business.

I want to do everything I can to help bring Melody and Jackson's killer to justice, who I'm almost certain now is Brandon, so I immediately agreed to help. Belle, however, didn't like the idea when I first told her about it, and she still doesn't like it.

"I still think it's dangerous," she grumbles as she hands me my garment bag. I wish Ren was here to distract her, but he's in a meeting in one of the back rooms right now. He understands why I want to do this and played a key part in getting Belle to agree to design my and Noah's costumes for the party.

Halloween is in full swing in my sister's store. Orange and black curly streamers hang from the ceiling. Cute ceramic ghosts and pumpkins are strategically placed on the racks and shelves. All of them have a friendly reminder attached to them that a discount will be applied if their purchase is over $100.

It's almost time for Belle to open the store, and I've already spotted a few people "casually" waiting outside. I'm surprised she found time to put together my and Noah's costumes. I know they would never expect it, but I'm going to get her and Ren a big gift for Christmas.

"You know why I need to do this," I say, folding the bag over my arm.

"You don't *need* to do this. Besides, one of the reasons you're doing this is to be close to Noah," she points out.

That *is* one of the reasons why I'm doing this, but I'll never admit it aloud.

"How does that work anyway? Did he need to get approval for you to go undercover with him? Did you have to sign something?" she asks.

I'm saved from answering her because someone knocks on the front door and asks if she's going to open soon. I scurry out the back exit, ignoring her request to call her later tonight.

I rush back home, noticing that the sky is dark gray and the clouds hang lower than usual – the perfect setting for Halloween. We have a half day at work today. The CEO loves Halloween and is hosting a big bash at his home this year. He invited all of us, but I politely declined, stating that I already had plans, although I would've declined if I hadn't had plans. This is the first time in a long time I'll be going out on Halloween.

As I expected, the day goes by fast. The last 30 minutes are filled with a company meeting. As everyone discusses their plans for the weekend, Avery chimes in.

"I'll be visiting my sister in Georgia. She's a party planner and she's hosting a birthday party for a millionaire, and she was able to snag an invitation for me!"

"Oh, how fun! I live in Georgia," I say. She giggles and nods.

"I remember! We should meet up for drinks, though I'm pretty sure my boyfriend won't approve of that."

"It's good to hear that you're back together! If you don't mind me asking, why wouldn't he approve?" I ask. Maybe he's really concerned about her safety? Or maybe she's had issues with alcohol in the past?

"He's very big on safety. He constantly reminds me to take care of myself, and he's very protective of me," she says, looking dreamily into the distance.

"And it's not official that we're back together, but he told me he's almost ready, so I'm over the moon. It's just such a fun time!" she chirps as she adjusts her glasses.

It crosses my mind that her boyfriend's controlling her and she's too in love with him to see it, but she doesn't look like she's being abused. Would I sense that? Even though I interact with my co-workers remotely, I still pick up things from them sometimes.

Her glasses stand out to me again and I start to wonder why, but I quickly realize it's because of their style. It reminds me of the 80s. Is Avery involved in Noah's case in some way? Is her boyfriend one of the thieves? Is she going to Brandon's party? I know it's a stretch to assume these things just because of her glasses, but I don't think it's a coincidence.

"Avery, if you don't mind me asking, who is the millionaire?"

"Oh! I don't remember his name, but I can get my invitation...," she trails off, shuffling through some papers on her desk.

"No, that's okay. I was just curious," I say. Now that I think about it, I don't think she's talking about Brandon. He's not a millionaire, and his wife isn't hosting a birthday party.

WHEN I DREAM OF YOU

As soon as I'm off work, I head to my closet to admire Belle's handiwork. I carefully unzip the garment bag and lay my costume on my bed. Sadness courses through me for a moment.

She recreated the outfit from my first dream perfectly.

Acid wash jeans with tiny sparkles on the pockets and near the hems. An off-the-shoulder short sleeve dark purple top. A soft sweep of ruffles starts on the left side near the waist and ends on the right just above the hip. Three bangles – lime green, dandelion yellow, and neon pink – are in a plastic bag along with large gold hoop earrings and a delicate gold necklace.

I smile. No way would my sister forget the jewelry. She argues that it's the most important part of an outfit. Well, that and hair. She's coming by tomorrow to help me with my hair and makeup.

I hope she doesn't ask again how the undercover process works. Noah didn't get approval for me to help him. None of his superiors know we're doing this, which means we're on our own. We need a confession from Brandon tomorrow.

Bruce strides into my room as I'm placing my costume back in the garment bag.

"What do you think, Bruce? Is this too dangerous?" I ask. He sits and wags his tail, gazing cheerfully at me. I take that as a sign that he doesn't agree with Belle.

After I give him a snack, I scoop him up, sit crisscrossed on the sofa, and place him in my lap. As I pet him, I turn on the TV and search for the music video for Richard Marx's song, "Right Here Waiting".

I now know why I sensed sadness from Sophie and why this song popped into my mind when I woke up from the last dream I had of Melody and Jackson.

Noah told me there was another reason why that song came to me. When he was hanging out with Jake, the song came on the radio. Jake made an offhand comment about how much Brandon had creeped him out. When Noah pressed him about it, he told him the full story.

Brandon was playing the song on a record player when Jake visited him. He was drunk, so Jake didn't want to disturb him too much, but Brandon kept talking about how much he missed the melody. Could Jake forgive him for killing the melody, even though it wasn't his fault? No, it wasn't really his fault that the melody was dead.

Chapter 12

October 30

Brandon and his wife, Melissa, live in an actual mansion. The foyer is as big as my apartment. Moonlight shines through the large rectangular windows that flank the front double doors. Starting at the entrance of the foyer and following the curve of both staircases – one to my left and one to my right – are black candleholders with white candles. They cast long shadows on the walls.

"Ready?" Noah whispers in my ear as people walk past us, murmuring excitedly. The warmth of his breath sends a tingle through me. His cologne smells like lavender and fresh earth – the promise of a new beginning.

He slides his hand in mine. Thankfully, I don't become drowsy with desire. I think it's because I can't feel his entire hand. I didn't tell Belle how I feel every time Noah touches me, but I'm glad she added black fingerless leather gloves to his outfit.

I squeeze his hand gently. He smiles softly. His look of admiration is back, but it feels different than last time. It's like he and I are the only people here – as if I'm some rare jewel he's found.

I've never liked being the center of attention, especially when my hair has been freeze sprayed into an 80s hairstyle and I have on colorful eyeshadow and bright pink lipstick. I blush and look away.

Out of the corner of my eye, I see Noah's smile falter. He clears his throat. "Okay, here we go."

We walk straight ahead, following the crowd. Costumes range from sophisticated vampires to Egyptian kings and queens to flower fairies to classy old-school detectives. I look at my costume and Noah's. He's wearing Jackson's outfit from my first dream. We're definitely underdressed, but we did this on purpose. Noah hopes we can guilt Brandon into confessing or giving up the real killer. I pointed out that Brandon may not have seen Melody in this outfit, but Noah said there's a reason I dreamt these outfits in detail.

I sneak a glance at his biceps. He has on a slim-fitting black muscle shirt. Belle added tiny sparkles near the hem of his shirt to match the sparkles on my pants. His ripped acid wash jeans are also fitted to his body, and his piercings complete the 80s rocker look.

We enter what I assume is a banquet hall. A massive ink black table adorned with décor and filled with fancy food is at the center of the room. Small round burgundy tables with dark floral arrangements and cauldrons overflowing with dry ice line the room. Dark pink velvet curtains cover the large windows, draping onto the floor in graceful piles. An eerie moving backdrop covers the wall across from us.

Waiters glide through the crowd, offering drinks. Wine glasses with gold bones for stems are filled to the brim. It's a small party. I'd say no more than 50 people are here, but

Brandon and Melissa aren't among them. While everyone mingles, Noah and I walk around the room, admiring the décor.

The floral arrangements on the burgundy tables are spooky beautiful – faux spiderwebs draped across black flowers and gold pumpkins. Silver skeleton heads, jeweled crowns, and glittery spiders decorate the dining table. Delicious food that I've seen on menus for extremely high prices are piled high on three tier silver trays. Dinner plates, goblets, and utensils have been laid out with a place card in front of each set. I find my name: "Melody". Noah's not using Jackson's name nor is he using his undercover name, Eli, in case Brandon has heard of it. He chose his surname, Everett, instead.

I find Sophie's name a few seats down. Sadness pricks my heart. She told us she wasn't going to attend, but I guess she didn't inform Melissa.

The eerie moving backdrop on the wall is a simulation of a foggy entrance of a cemetery. Dark clouds roll through the sky. The headstones cast slanted shadows on the ground. A rat enters the cemetery and scurries across, disappearing behind the last headstone.

I know Brandon may not have planned the party, but it angers me to see this. How can he be so callous about Melody and Jackson's murder, especially when he pulled the trigger? Sure, he felt guilty when he was drunk, but even then the truth didn't come out.

"Hey," Noah says. His voice, low and warm, calms me immediately. I look into his eyes, which are filled with concern.

"Do you want to leave?" he asks.

"No, I'm fine," I say, smiling to reassure him. He studies me for a moment then nods and looks behind me.

"Here they are," he whispers.

Brandon was 18 at the time of Melody and Jackson's murder, which means he's in his 50s now. Melissa has kept up with herself, but he hasn't. He looks worn down and his skin is pale. He's far from the poised, handsome teenager he once was. I hope the part of him that loved Melody is still in him somewhere. Maybe that part will surface tonight and tell us the truth.

Brandon and Melissa's costumes complement each other like mine and Noah's do. They're dressed as a zombie king and queen. As they come closer, I start to tense up. I don't think I can talk to Brandon. I can't shake his hand. I can't look him in the eye. He took two promising young lives.

Nausea rolls through me. Brandon is the killer. I grip Noah's hand to steady myself, wishing I could tell him what I'm now certain of.

"You must be Melody and Everett, Sophie's Canadian friends. It's wonderful to meet you!" Melissa exclaims. Up close, you can tell she's an older woman, but her makeup is flawless and her eyes are bright. She extends her hand to me. Her nails are polished a shiny blood red. The color looks so familiar... but I can't remember where I've seen it.

"It's nice to meet you, Mrs. Adler," I say. She waves her free hand dismissively.

"Honey, don't call me that. I'm Melissa and this is my husband, Brandon," she says, nodding at Brandon. I can't bring myself to look at him, so I keep my focus on Melissa. As she shakes Noah's hand, she studies our outfits.

"What an interesting costume choice! Why the 80s? You both look too young to have lived during that time."

Noah laughs politely. "My mom was a teenager in the 80s. She showed me the music and movies she loved while I was growing up," he says. Melissa laughs and delicately places her hand on his shoulder, wiping off lint that I'm sure is not there.

"Well, you look fabulous. I can tell your outfits are custom-made like ours are. You'll have to give me the number to your designer." She turns her attention to Brandon.

"Darling, I completely forgot to tell you! Melody and Everett have built an extremely successful veterinarian franchise in Canada. They're looking to expand their business here and invest," she says. Brandon clears his throat.

"Melody?" he asks, looking straight at me. I can't put it off any longer. I look him in the eye.

A storm of guilt, shame, and sadness has been building up in him for years. He wants to scream so loud that the walls of his mansion come crashing down on him.

"Yes, sir," I say with as polite of an expression as I can make, but I don't smile. I don't feel sad for him. Melody and Jackson deserved to live.

"What a pretty name," he replies quietly. Melissa smiles, but it doesn't reach her eyes this time.

"Dinner will begin in a few minutes. Feel free to mingle until then. Excuse us," she says, patting Brandon's hand. He turns around slowly and trudges after her.

When they exit the banquet hall, Noah turns to me, but he doesn't have to say anything. I know what we need to do.

We quickly exit the hall and glance around the foyer. "They must've gone upstairs," I whisper.

"Which way?" he asks. I resist the urge to groan.

"I don't have the answers to everything. Maybe left?" I suggest. He winces.

"Right. Sorry. But I'm still going with what you said."

We head to the staircase on our left and race up the steps. When we reach the second floor, we're greeted by a long and silent dark hallway. Noah, still focused on the left side, grabs my hand and gently tugs me forward. The last dream I had of Melody and Jackson races through my mind. Jackson did the same thing right before Brandon chased them. I gasp and wrench my hand away, momentarily forgetting who and where I am. Noah whirls around.

"What's wrong?" he says, his voice a little too loud. I'm grateful for that, even if he didn't mean to do it, because it brings me back to reality.

"You just reminded me of my dream, but I'm okay now," I say.

"Are you sure?" he asks.

A sliver of light appears at the end of the hallway on our left, growing bigger by the second. I pull Noah toward the first room I see and twist the doorknob. Surprisingly, it opens. I keep the door cracked a bit so we can see what's happening.

Melissa rushes by, her heels clacking furiously down the stairs and across the foyer. We wait to see if Brandon passes by, but he doesn't. Noah opens the door a bit wider and we peek out. There's still light at the end of the hall.

Noah turns around to face me. "I can take it from here," he says. I shake my head.

"No, I can do this," I reply firmly. He smiles wide.

"Follow my lead."

When we're near the room the light is coming from, Noah says in a loud voice, "Babe, I don't think we're anywhere near the restrooms. Can't it wait? Dinner's going to start soon."

I match his volume. "I'm sure I'll find them any second now. Why don't you wait for me downstairs? Oh, look! Maybe there's someone in there who can help me."

I push the door open. Brandon is sitting behind a desk. His chair is angled toward the empty fireplace. An empty liquor glass is in his hand and a beautifully carved glass bottle of liquor is sitting open on his desk. He's staring blankly into the fireplace. When he notices us, he jumps up. I giggle.

"I'm sorry, Mr. Adler! I didn't mean to scare you. My husband and I are trying to find the bathroom. Can you please show us where it is?" He looks stunned and Noah takes the opportunity.

"Look, babe! Isn't this beautiful?" he says.

Beside a bookshelf is a record player on top of a small table.

"Mr. Adler, where do you keep your records? I'd love to look at your collection," Noah says.

"They're in there," Brandon mumbles, pointing at the bookshelf. All I see are thick books with gold spines. His records must be at the bottom, behind the small glass double doors. Brandon sets his liquor glass on the desk.

"We should be getting back to the party. My wife doesn't like tardiness," he says, starting for the door. Noah crouches down so that he's at eye level with the glass doors.

"Do you have the record of – Oh, what's the name of that song? It's one of my mom's favorites. Babe, do you know which one I'm talking about?" Noah asks.

"Oh, yes! It's one of my favorites too. 'Right Here Waiting,'" I say. From the corner of my eye, I see Brandon freeze. Noah snaps his fingers.

"That's it! Do you remember who sang it? Wasn't his first name Jackson?" he asks. I start to respond, but Brandon interrupts.

"What are you doing? Who are you?" he asks, his voice shaky. He takes several steps back and bumps into the fireplace mantel. The picture frames on the mantel rattle. His eyes are wide with fear.

Several seconds of silence follow. It feels like the air is weighted.

Noah carefully slides his hand under the hem of his jeans and pulls out a small silver gun. He stands up slowly, keeping his hand behind his back.

"Mr. Adler, I think you know," Noah says, his voice quiet but firm. He has that discerning look I find so attractive, though it's obvious Brandon finds it nothing but unnerving.

"W-Who are you?" he whispers. He stumbles toward his desk. Noah angles his body so that he's blocking me from Brandon, but I can still see what's happening.

"It-it can't be. Leave me alone!" Brandon shouts. He fumbles with one of the desk drawers. Noah aims the gun at him.

"Mr. Adler, I suggest you keep your hands where I can see them," he says. He's so steady, so calm. It helps keep my nerves at bay.

Brandon freezes again, his eyes flickering from Noah to the desk drawer. After a few seconds, his eyes land on me. His bottom lip trembles and he collapses into his chair. He begins to cry quietly. Noah moves closer, keeping his gun trained on him.

"I'm sorry. I'm so sorry," Brandon wails.

"Why are you sorry, Mr. Adler?" Noah asks, his voice a bit softer.

"I'm sorry for everything," Brandon whispers. A strange, cold *click* sounds behind me. I turn around and yelp when I see Melissa aiming a gun at me.

"That's *enough*," she hisses. Noah spins around and she *tsks*.

"Honey, don't do that. I'll kill your pretty wife." She places a hand on her hip and laughs. "I thought there was something strange about you two, but I'm sure we can work something out to make you go away quietly."

"So it was you," Noah says. She smiles. A chill crawls down my spine. This is what it's like to look into the eyes of someone without remorse. It explains why I didn't sense anything from her earlier.

"No, it was my father-in-law, but I had the pleasure of watching."

My fear disappears as I remember a small detail from my first dream. A detail I had completely forgotten until now.

"You must be the one Brandon kissed. The one that caused Melody to break up with him," I say. For a moment, she's taken aback.

"How did you know that?" she asks. I ignore her and continue.

"So Brandon's father found out that Jackson had Brandon's watch. He couldn't risk Jackson turning it in to the police, so he tried to bribe Jackson into giving him the watch. When

Jackson refused, he killed him and Melody. But that doesn't explain how you ended up witnessing it," I say.

Melissa stammers for a response, lowering her gun a bit. Noah lunges at her. She screams as they fall. Their guns skid across the floor.

"Let me go!" she screeches, wrestling underneath Noah. I look around to see where Noah's gun went. Brandon appears at my side, aiming Noah's gun at her. She stops struggling when she notices him.

"That's enough, *darling*," he snaps.

Noah cuffs Melissa and pulls her to her feet. Her eyes narrow as she and Brandon continue to stare each other down.

"You never stopped loving her," she hisses. Brandon doesn't respond. His eyes are hard and he's clutching Noah's gun so tight that his knuckles are white.

Noah glances at both of them. After a few seconds, he takes out his cell phone. As he calls for backup, Brandon starts speaking to me, but his eyes never leave Melissa.

"I've felt her with me at times, you know. Melody, I mean. I didn't pull the trigger, but I may as well have. I knew my father was involved, but I didn't know Melissa witnessed it until now. Does that make me an accessory? Not that it matters. I'm going to jail anyway. I know I deserve it. I've done things I'm not proud of to keep my father's business going." He chuckles without humor. "I've always done what he's told me to do."

"Like robbing jewelry stores and art museums so your father's business wouldn't fail like it almost did when you were in high school?" I ask. He looks at me surprised.

Melissa screams and elbows Noah, stumbling as she tries to get away. Noah staggers back but grabs her before she can run out the door and throws her to the ground. Brandon rushes closer to them.

"Shut up and don't move," he growls. Melissa doesn't respond. She looks dazed. I get the feeling she's always been the one to throw people to the ground – metaphorically and physically.

Noah finds Melissa's gun and tucks it behind his back in the waistline of his jeans. "I'll take it from here, Mr. Adler," he says, reaching for his gun. Brandon reluctantly hands it over and sits on the floor, far away from Melissa. Noah keeps a watchful eye on them.

"Mr. Adler, I'm Detective Everett and, in addition to solving the murders of Melody Wilde and Jackson Stone, I've come to place you under arrest," he says. Brandon shrugs.

"Sure, but I'll only speak to her," he says, nodding at me. Noah shakes his head.

"I'll be taking your confession."

"I'll only talk to her," Brandon says. Noah moves closer to me.

"Do you mind?" he asks in a low voice. I glance at Brandon who's staring at me quizzically. I realize I misinterpreted the nausea I felt earlier. *He* was the one who was nauseous. He was sick from knowing his father was a killer and for keeping quiet about it all this time.

I guess Sophie was right. Brandon really did love Melody, but he wasn't strong enough to go against his father.

Noah's second theory was right after all. He guessed that Brandon's father was the killer, but he didn't anticipate Melissa being a witness.

After Brandon spoke to me, I learned a few things. The robbery of Jackson's father's store was the first time Brandon took part in his father's crimes. He confirmed that Jackson's father's death was an accident.

Brandon was the getaway driver, but he had decided to step out of the car for a few minutes. As he was messing with his watch, he heard a gunshot and stumbled back to the car. His watch fell off, but he didn't notice it until it was too late.

Brandon's description of that night matched the sounds I heard at the robbery I witnessed – glass shattering, shouting, and a high-pitched alarm ringing. Since Noah described the robbery he was a part of as a silent crime, I realized that I had heard the past – the robbery Brandon took part in.

Brandon's father told him what happened one year after Melody and Jackson's murder. To this day, Brandon doesn't know why he told him because he never suspected him.

His father had gone back to the jewelry store to look for Brandon's watch. When he didn't find it, he assumed someone had picked it up. He came across Melody and Jackson at the ice cream parlor and saw Jackson showing the watch to Melody. He tried to bribe Jackson into giving him Brandon's watch. When Jackson refused, he snapped and killed them and had a friend who was a police officer cover it up so their deaths would remain unsolved.

As to how Melissa ended up witnessing the crime, I don't think we'll ever know. She refused to speak, even to Noah. I have my own theory, though, based on what I saw in my dream:

She was the person painted in blood red, seated a few booths away from Melody and Jackson. She saw them talking to Brandon's father and witnessed them running away. She followed them and saw the murder.

Was it a coincidence that she married Brandon? I don't think so. I think Brandon's father found out she witnessed the crime and offered to help her marry Brandon in exchange for her silence.

As for the robberies, Brandon did what his father had taught him to do. If the business was in danger of failing, he was to rob jewelry stores and art museums across the U.S. After some time passed, he would have his men sell the items to the highest international bidder on the black market. The money would be routed to several different international accounts. It would then be cashed and delivered to Brandon's doorstep by various international airlines.

"How do you feel after everything that's happened tonight?" Noah asks.

We're nearing my front door. It's a bit past midnight, which means it's officially Halloween. The evening air is cool and laced with sweet-smelling laundry detergent.

"I'm relieved, actually. Melody and Jackson can be at peace now," I say. Noah smiles and shifts his stance slightly. Under the bright lights of our apartment walkway, he looks different. He's still gorgeous, but the 80s outfit doesn't quite fit him, which makes sense because it's a costume, but there's something else. Something I can't figure out.

"That's exactly how I feel when I solve a case," he says. His smile fades into a solemn, grateful expression.

"Layla, I cannot thank you enough for how much you helped me. Your bravery is beautiful."

I blush. "Thank you," I say. I turn to open my door, and he starts to speak so fast that, for a second, I wonder if I imagined it.

"What I mean is you are beautiful. Will you go out with me tomorrow night? I mean, today. This evening."

This is the part where I should say something sexy or witty. A simple enthusiastic "Yes!" would suffice. Instead, I ask, "Go out?"

Noah's neck and cheeks turn red. "Yes. Go out on a date."

"Okay," I say, not sounding enthusiastic at all. I hope I sound shocked. Which I am. I can't believe he's asked me out on a date when I look like I just finished shooting a commercial for freeze hairspray.

Noah beams. "Really?"

How could any woman refuse that smile?

"Yes," I say, smiling wide.

"I'll see you tonight at seven," he says. He starts to walk to his apartment.

"Wait! Where are we going? How should I dress?" I ask. He turns around, grinning like he's won a prize.

"Anything! You always look beautiful."

If I wasn't falling in love with him before, I most certainly am now.

Chapter 13: Dream

I'm in a school gym. The lights are dim and music is playing. To my right is a refreshment table. A clear plastic bowl filled with fruit punch and plastic cups stacked beside it are on top of the table. Confetti is scattered across the gym floor. A large banner is taped on the wall across from me, announcing a spring formal.

Is this where Noah has taken me for our date? No, that can't be right. We're not in high school.

Giggling and shouts of joy erupt from behind me. Melody and Jackson are dressed for the formal and they're dancing. She squeals as he dips her low. He laughs, pulls her up, and pecks her on the lips. Luna runs around them, barking playfully. Melody notices me standing a few feet away and gasps.

"Layla!" she exclaims and runs toward me. She crashes into me and hugs me tight. She pulls away and smiles. There are tears in her eyes.

"I'm so happy you're here! Thank you for everything," she says, pulling me in for another hug. I don't speak because I'm afraid I'll burst into tears.

When she lets go, Jackson smiles and tilts his head toward me as a show of respect. "Thank you, Layla. I appreciate everything you've done for us," he says. It's the first time I've heard him speak.

His voice is soft and sweet. He closes the distance between us and kisses me on the top of my head. It reminds me of the way a father would kiss his daughter.

How would their lives have turned out? Would they have gotten married and had kids? Would they have grandchildren by now? Would they have been happy?

"You're welcome," I say, my voice cracking on the last word.

Melody gives me a sympathetic look and shakes her head. "Don't cry for us, Layla. We're happy."

She places her hands on my shoulders, looking at me the way my mom has done when she's needed to tell me something extremely important. "We'll be watching over you, okay?"

I smile and wipe away my tears.

"One last thing. Please close your eyes," she says.

I don't want this to be goodbye, but I do what she says. She turns me around gently. Jackson's voice drifts by my ear.

"It's not what you think."

Luna barks and the music fades. My vision goes dark, alerting me that the lights have turned off. Ice-cold air rushes by me. Goosebumps flare up on my arms, and the hair on the back of my neck stands up. I gasp and open my eyes.

I'm in a small gray room. Hundreds of photos are taped to the walls, but they're blurry. The carpet is worn and dirty. A small window faces me. Bleak sunlight streams in. Someone sobs softly behind me.

I turn around and see a woman curled up in a corner of the room.

"Why did you do this?" she asks between sobs, wiping the mucus that's coming out of her nose with her sleeve.

Her black hair hangs a little past her shoulders. Her eyes are hazel and red around the rims. Her arms are wrapped tight around her legs, but I can tell she's curvy.

"Why?" she screams. I take a step back.

"What did I do?" I ask. She sucks in a breath and looks behind me. The fear in her eyes makes my stomach sink. I slowly turn around.

Noah is pointing a gun at me. He has a look in his eyes that I've never seen before. It's as if he has to do this – as if I'm a criminal that must be stopped. What's more disturbing than that is the gun he's holding. It's bright red.

"I'll make it quick," he says. My vision blurs until I can only see the barrel of the gun.

The gunshot rattles my bones and makes my ears ring. I don't have to see the wound to know I'm dead.

Chapter 14

After I got a few hours of sleep, I visited Belle and Ren, who were anxious to find out what had happened. They gasped in all the right places and waited until I was finished to ask questions. I was careful not to mention my ability so Ren wouldn't be confused, though my resolve to keep him in the dark is waning now that Noah knows. Maybe Ren will believe too.

As to be expected, Belle was furious when I admitted that Noah and I went rogue, but her anger vanished when I told her about my date tonight.

"Ahh!" she screams in delight, jumping up from her chair. "What are you going to wear? I can help you. It's been a while since I've checked out your closet anyway," she says as she bounces to the door.

Seeing her excited for me reminds me of Sophie and how she looked when she talked about Melody. I know I shouldn't be sad, but it's not Melody and Jackson I'm sad for.

I'm sad for Sophie and every other loved one they left behind.

I run to Belle and wrap my arms around her. I don't like expressing my emotions aloud, so I tell her that I'll always love her through my hug. That I'm thankful for every time she's been there for me. That even though she and I are completely different, we are somehow exactly the same.

She gasps and softly pats my back. "What's wrong, honey?"

I want to tell her about my dream, but I can't. I'm not in denial. I'm just frightened by my way of thinking. It's like I'm telling her goodbye.

I tried to hide what was bothering me, but Belle forced it out of me when we were alone. I contemplated canceling my date with Noah, but Belle forbade me to. I know that sounds silly because how can my sister forbid me to do something? I'm a grown woman, for goodness' sake. But no one dares to cross Belle when she gets that look in her eye and uses her commanding tone of voice.

She kept reminding me what Jackson said as she helped me get ready. *It's not what you think.* Even with that in mind, I can't bring myself to be excited. Belle snaps her fingers in my face. I hate it when she does that, but it always works.

"Stop that," I snap.

"You forced me to," she shoots back. Then she smiles and assesses my outfit.

"You look beautiful."

I can't help but reciprocate her smile. "Thank you," I murmur. She turns around and enters my closet, resuming her bossy tone.

"Now for the shoes. Honestly, Layla, if I left it up to you, you'd always be in sweatshirts and jeans."

I roll my eyes as she continues her criticism of my wardrobe. Belle's sweet moments never last long, but I know she means well. It's kind of funny how she and I can go from sweet to snappy within seconds. I bite my lip to keep from laughing.

Bruce enters my room and heads straight to my closet. He starts licking Belle's leg and she screams. I can't hold in my laughter any longer. Bruce thinks we're playing and runs around Belle, who gently pushes him away every time he tries to lick her.

It almost makes me forget about my dream. Almost.

Seven o'clock comes faster than I anticipate. I'm standing outside my front door, watching storm clouds drift by. My nerves are bundled tight and my muscles are coiled, as if I'm preparing to run. I picture myself racing down the stairs and going... Where?

Images of different landscapes flood my mind, but I force my imagination to stop. My mind is in "fight or flight" mode, so I remind myself of what Jackson said. I didn't see the actual future. Noah would never harm me.

I need to stop panicking. Maybe I should tell him my dream...

Someone touches my shoulder from behind and I whirl around. Noah holds up his hands and takes a step back.

"I'm sorry! I didn't mean to scare you," he says. I stammer for a response, finally settling for a lame "It's okay". I quickly bury my nerves and smile, although I can tell he isn't buying it.

"What's wrong?" he asks, his brows furrowing as he studies me. I gulp.

"Nothing," I say in a too bright voice. Noah gives me a pointed look and crosses his arms.

"I had a dream," I mumble. I expect him to be a bit exasperated and ask if we can talk about it after our date.

"Oh? What about?" he asks, looking genuinely interested. He's surprised me yet again.

But I don't feel like explaining it. I don't want to dampen our date by telling him that he killed me in my dream.

Now I'm irritated with myself. I should've been paying attention to my surroundings. I would've seen Noah coming and we wouldn't be having this conversation right now.

"Can we talk about it later tonight?" I ask. He smiles and nods.

"Sure! I thought of a few things we could do, but I want us to decide together, especially since you know the area more than I do."

He lists his ideas as we head to his car. All of them sound good to me, so I tell him he can choose.

"Are you sure?" he asks as he opens the passenger door for me. That's when I notice what he's wearing – a dark green V-neck T-shirt and dark blue jeans. It's so simple yet beautiful. It complements my black T-shirt and dark green bohemian skirt. The color of his shirt reminds me of the forest woven throughout the city. He fits in perfectly with the landscape – alluring and strong.

I take a step closer. His lips are about an inch from mine. His eyes widen and his cheeks slowly turn red. I didn't know I had this effect on him.

"So long as I'm with you, it doesn't matter where we go or what we do," I say. I have no idea where this confidence is coming from, but I like it. Noah doesn't say anything. He just stares. After a few seconds, he closes the car door and offers his hand to me.

"Come with me," he says. I slide my hand in his without hesitation. A beautiful collision of color floods my vision. It delights me to know that something so beautiful exists, even if it's just my imagination. Unless it's not my imagination and what I saw came from Noah. But what does it mean?

I squeal as Noah spins me around his living room. Waltz music plays on his TV, our laughter in stark contrast to it. He's been trying to teach me a dance his parents learned on their first date. I'm pretty sure they were more graceful than me. I busted out laughing when Noah stared dramatically into my eyes.

Bruce stands on his hind legs, pawing at the air, his tongue lolling out of his mouth. I'm surprised he's so cheerful. The storm hasn't hit yet, but there's been some thunder and lightning. Maybe he's distracted by the commotion Noah and I are making.

Before Noah and I went to his apartment, he asked if I wanted to bring Bruce. He reminded me of the storm that's approaching and remembered that Bruce doesn't like to be alone during this kind of weather.

Noah's laughter tickles my ear. My back is against his chest. One of his hands is on my stomach and the other is on my waist, steadying me. "Ready for one more spin?" he whispers.

It's hard to explain, but I *feel* him. His breath, his warmth, his hands on my body. I'm getting hotter by the second. His breathing starts to match mine – shallow and fast.

I can't initiate a kiss. It'd be too embarrassing if he said he wanted to take it slow.

"Can we sit down?" I ask, stepping away from him.

He clears his throat and tries to smile. Does that mean I should have kissed him? It's too late now. The tension between us is fading.

I try to remember the last time I felt this way – nervous and out of breath and delirious with desire. Sure, I've crushed on guys before and have been excited when I've gone out on dates, but it's different with Noah. I think it's because he knows about my ability. I feel more open with him than I have with any other guy I've dated.

He pushes aside the TV trays we were eating on so we can sit on the sofa. He offered to cook me dinner, but he realized he hadn't been grocery shopping in a while and only had frozen dinners. It was the best frozen dinner I've ever eaten, but I'll never tell him that. I don't want him to think I'm just saying that to be nice, and I definitely don't want him to think I'm making fun of him.

Bruce must sense the mood change because he heads over to us for a quick rub on the head then rounds the edge of the sofa and disappears.

Noah takes my hands and gently pulls me toward him. I hesitate and he picks up on it.

"Oh, I'm sorry," he says, releasing my hands. I snatch his hands back.

"No, it's okay! You just catch me off guard sometimes," I say. Why did I just admit that aloud? Noah smiles his boyish, slightly sheepish smile.

"I catch you off guard? What exactly do you mean?" he asks. He intertwines his fingers with mine. I suck in a breath.

"You're just so gorgeous," I say. He laughs. Why am I saying these things aloud?

"Well, it's true. Have you looked in a mirror lately?" I mumble. He scoots closer to me and withdraws one of his hands from mine. He touches my shoulder then softly brushes back my hair. The collision of color I saw earlier tonight explodes in my mind.

"I appreciate the compliment, Layla, but you are the beautiful one," he says, his voice dropping to a husky whisper. Now I know why Sophie looked at us the way she did when we visited her. I can see it now.

In some ways, Noah and I are parallels of Jackson and Melody. It's hard to explain, and I don't know how or why, but it may be why I was able to communicate directly with them in my last dream.

I close my eyes as Noah leans forward. He brushes his lips against mine. When our eyes flutter open, I'm starstruck by the emotion in his eyes. If I was disoriented before, I don't know how to describe what I feel now. It's like he's flooding my veins, turning my blood into fire then ice then back to fire, all within seconds. How do I make this stop? Do I want it to stop?

He kisses me this time – eager, hungry kisses. When he presses his body against mine, I figure out what he wants. I lie down and he settles himself between my legs. Does he want to have sex?

He's running his hands all over my body. His lips make their way down my neck. He pulls down the neckline of my shirt and gently kisses my bare shoulder.

I start to speak, but his lips are back on mine again. My thoughts are chaotic. I feel like I have the best kind of fever. I would've never guessed Noah was so aggressive. It's as if he can't get enough of me. When our tongues meet, his voice enters my mind. *This is how you make me feel.* He's never said that to me before, so I don't get it at first. Then it clicks.

Everything I've felt when he has touched me has been from him. *I* make him delirious. It's extremely flattering, but I have one question for him before we can continue.

When his lips find my neck again, I suck in a breath. "Noah?" I gasp.

"Yeah," he whispers between kisses.

"Wait, please," I say, placing my hand on his shoulder and gently pushing him away. He immediately jerks back.

"No, no! It's okay," I say, pulling him toward me. He relaxes a bit.

"I need to ask you something before we go any further. Do you only like me because of what I can do?"

He looks at me confused. "For what you can do?" His eyes widen in realization.

"Oh, I see. Your gift."

He smiles and lightly touches my lips. His fingers trail down to my bare shoulder.

His touch is a whisper, a promise. He grabs a lock of my hair, rubbing it between his forefinger and thumb.

"I like all of you, Layla. What you can do intrigues me and I am attracted to you even more because of it, but I liked you before I knew about your gift."

I remember the first two times I felt his attraction to me. He didn't know about my gift then. He's telling the truth.

I smile and lean in to kiss him, but he averts his gaze. Remorse covers his face.

"Layla, there's something I need to tell you. I –"

A knock on the front door interrupts him. His attention snaps to the door.

"Are you expecting someone?" I ask. He shakes his head and slowly gets up from the sofa. I reach for the remote to turn down the volume on the TV, but he shakes his head furiously.

"Let it play," he mouths. The knocking comes harder this time. I flinch. A chill like the one I felt in my dream races down my spine. My mouth goes dry and my heart begins to beat so fast that it feels like it's trying to bust out of my ribcage. I struggle to catch a breath.

Noah tiptoes to his desk. He pulls out a gun from underneath, crouches down, and motions me to join him. When I'm beside him, I gasp. *Bruce.*

"I need to get Bruce," I say. Noah grabs my hand.

"He'll be fine. Stay here," he whispers fiercely.

I've only seen Noah this way once, and that was during the robbery. Everyone involved in the heists has been taken into custody. Could this be a family member or a friend who's seeking revenge?

The knocking is so strong that I'm sure whoever is outside is going to bust down the door at any moment. Noah grimaces.

"Who is it?" he calls out.

No one responds.

"Who is it?" he shouts.

"You know," a woman's voice says. I recognize that voice. Before I can tell Noah I know who it is, a burst of white light blinds me. A police siren wails so loud that my ears ache. As the siren fades, a street materializes and two figures – one male and one female – appear on it, walking. The man looks over his shoulder as the woman follows him, taking dozens of photos. When the man turns back around, his features appear, allowing me to see his identity.

It's Noah.

"Avery," Noah says, as if he's reprimanding a child. She screams and the door bangs open.

I scramble to get up. Noah is already on his feet, blocking me from her. He's holding his gun behind his back.

"Avery, how did you find me?" he asks softly.

"Don't talk to me like that!" she screams. She slams the door shut. Great. Now we're locked inside with her.

I glance at my phone, which is perched on top of the TV tray a few feet away. It's too far away. I discreetly look around for Bruce, but he's nowhere in sight. I hope he stays wherever he's at and doesn't make any noise.

Avery is pacing in the entryway. She's short and slim. Her long red hair is unkempt and frizzy. Her eyes are red around the rims and her face is blotchy. It looks like she's been crying.

"Avery, why don't we sit down?" Noah says. She stops and stares at him with a wild look in her eyes.

"Sit down? You want me to sit down? After what you've just done to me, you want me to sit down?" she asks, her voice rising until she's screeching at the top of her lungs.

I start to hope that someone will hear the commotion and call in a noise disturbance. Then I remember it's Halloween. They might think it's a prank.

"You're right. I'm sorry. What would you like to do?" Noah asks, his voice smooth but strained. She thrusts her arm forward, pointing a little away from him.

"I want to talk to *her*," she snaps. My stomach drops. Me? What did I do?

My last question helps me understand who Avery is. She doesn't look like her, but she's the woman from my dream – the one Melody and Jackson showed me.

Noah becomes rigid. "She has nothing to do with this," he says.

Avery laughs darkly. "Then why is she hiding behind you like a coward?"

I slowly step out from behind Noah.

"Hi, Avery," I say. I don't know how my voice is so steady when the rest of me feels like I've just taken a bath in ice water, but I'm glad I sound strong.

Her nose scrunches up and turns red. She wipes away her tears with the sleeve of her shirt.

"I thought you were my friend," she cries. Out of the corner of my eye, I see Noah glance at me in shock.

"I am your friend," I say.

"No, you're not! You wouldn't be with Noah if you were my friend! He's my boyfriend," she says, her voice cracking on the last word.

"I'm so sorry, Avery. Noah didn't tell me you were together. I would've never gone out with him if I knew," I say. That seems to calm her down some.

"Really?" she asks. I try to smile.

"I would never hurt a friend," I say. She smiles and for a moment, I think she's going to be okay. Then her eyes widen, as if she's remembering something.

"No, I saw the way he looked at you," she says softly, her expression dazed.

This is not good. I should keep her talking so Noah can think of a way to get us out of here safely.

"What do you mean?" I ask. Avery gasps and places her hands over her mouth. She's looking behind me. I don't turn around in case it's a trick, but I don't think it is. She has a glisten in her eyes that makes me believe she's far away from reality.

"Yes, that's right... I was going to surprise him today. I wanted to let him know I had officially moved here when I saw him outside with you. He was looking at you like...," she trails off, her hands dropping to her sides.

"Like what?" I ask gently. She looks at me and her expression darkens.

"Like no one else existed," she snaps. She reaches from behind her and pulls out a gun from the back of her pants.

This is the second time in 24 hours I've had a gun aimed at me. I thought Melissa was scary, but she's got nothing on Avery.

Avery clicks the safety lock off. "I'm sorry, but no one will come between me and Noah. I know you're my friend, so I'll make it quick."

Noah is aiming his gun at her and he starts to say something, but he's interrupted by a sharp cry from her.

"Get it off! Get it off!" she yowls, shaking her right leg. Bruce is clinging onto her ankle. His teeth are clenched in her so tight that blood is seeping out of the sides of his mouth. She points her gun at Bruce.

"No!" I scream, lunging at her. Noah yanks me back. A gun goes off. Avery's screaming stops.

There's a hole in the center of her chest, and blood is slowly spilling out. Avery coughs and looks at us with a pained expression. She drops her gun. Bruce lets go of her. He runs toward me as she crumples to the floor.

Noah looks like he's frozen in place. He's still aiming his gun at her. His muscles are taut and he's staring at her with a hard glint in his eyes.

Warmth wells up in me. I'm sure he'd protect anyone who's in harm's way, but I feel like he would've done anything to keep me alive. Was Avery right about what she saw? Is Noah falling in love with me?

She places her hand over her wound. "Why?" she asks in a raspy voice.

"You left me no other choice," Noah replies quietly.

"But I love you," she whines.

His hard expression melts into sadness. He lowers his gun and shakes his head.

"That's not love, Avery," he sighs.

Her ragged breathing slows. After a few minutes, she becomes still. Noah slowly walks over to her. He kneels and places two fingers on her neck. After a few seconds, he lifts his fingers off her. He turns to me, his eyes full of guilt and shame.

"I'm so sorry, Layla," he whispers.

Chapter 15

December 20

Light streams in through my bedroom window, filling my room with a dreamy golden glow. Noah stirs beside me but doesn't wake. I want to run my hand through his hair and trace the shape of his lips, but he looks so peaceful when he sleeps. I don't want to wake him. I close my eyes, but sleep doesn't come, so I replay everything that's happened since I met Noah.

When I think about Avery, I feel a twinge of sadness. Noah met her a few months after he was promoted to detective. He found her behind a nightclub. Someone had stolen her purse and had brutally beaten her. After a couple weeks, Noah found the mugger, who was responsible for a string of robberies and beatings throughout the city.

Noah kept in touch with Avery after the mugger was arrested to make sure she was okay. After some time, she asked him out on a date. Since the case was closed, he thought it would be okay to accept.

After dating for a few months, he decided he didn't want to be in a serious relationship with her. He told her he wanted to focus on his career so he wouldn't hurt her feelings.

That's when Avery snapped.

She constantly harassed him and threatened any woman he dated through social media, texts, and calls. She lost weight and started growing out her hair. She told Noah she was molding herself into what she believed was his ideal woman.

Noah eventually put a restraining order on her. She was placed in a psychiatric facility soon after.

Noah tried to resume a normal life, but the ordeal had affected him. He was withdrawn and jumpy. Theo suggested therapy, but Noah didn't want to go that route. After a few weeks, his boss came to him with an alternative solution: Work undercover in Georgia. When Noah arrived here, he was still working on letting go of the trauma, which is why he was so cautious at first.

When he spoke with the psychiatric facility Avery was in, they explained she had successfully completed treatment and had been released in May, which was during the time he was in the process of going undercover.

Somehow, she found out he was going to Georgia and got a job with the company I work for. She really did have a master's degree in digital arts, but she had faked some of her job history and references. Noah explained to me how she did it, but I still can't believe she made it look so real.

She didn't lie about moving to Georgia. She had rented an apartment at our complex and was in the process of moving her things in. She must've seen Noah and me talking at his car before we went to his apartment.

She did lie about having one sister. She actually had three, but they were all estranged.

I know I shouldn't feel sorry for Avery, but I do. She really believed she loved Noah. I think that's why I didn't sense anything from her.

Noah was shocked to discover that Avery and I knew each other. He blamed himself for putting me in danger. I told him about the last dream I had of Melody and Jackson. If I had told him my dream earlier that evening, Avery might not have died. If anyone was to blame for what happened, it was me.

Noah told me to never think that way. If Avery had lived, I would've been in constant danger. He believes she had to die.

Last month, Noah resigned from the force. He told me he felt it was time to leave. He now works as an assistant security manager for a large corporation. I'm surprised they let him keep his piercings. I thought he would've taken them out a long time ago, but I'm not saying anything. The rocker look fits him.

My phone buzzes, alerting me to a text. I smile as I read Belle's message. Noah and I are going over to her and Ren's for dinner tonight. It's taking time for Belle to fully approve of Noah because of what happened, but she's warming up to him, much to his relief. As I'm texting her back, Noah stirs and opens his eyes. He smiles wide, as if he's just awoken to the best surprise of his life. He leans forward and kisses me slowly. His lips feel like fire – tantalizing yet warm and cozy.

"Good morning, Layla," he whispers. I love the way he says my name. It's like he's intoxicated by my presence. I laugh as he starts to tickle me, and I gently swat his hand away. He grins and lays back down.

Bruce enters the room, tongue lolling out of his mouth and his tail wagging hard. He stands on his hind legs and places his front paws on Noah's side of the bed.

"Well, good morning, Agent," Noah says. Bruce's tail wags harder and he paws at the bed. Noah's official nickname for him is "Secret Agent", but he shortens it to "Agent" sometimes. Bruce was so stealthy that night that I didn't notice him beside Avery until she cried out. I truly believe he was a secret agent in a past life.

When Bruce leaves, Noah turns his attention back to me and slowly trails his fingers up my arm. The sensation is excruciatingly wonderful. "How did you sleep?" he asks.

"Really, really good. I can't remember the last time I had a dreamless sleep. How about you?" I ask.

"I had a wonderful dream," he murmurs.

I run my hand through his hair. "What was it about?" I ask. He grabs my hand and kisses it. Then he shifts his body so that he's on top of me. We stay like that for a while, kissing and exploring each other's bodies. Even though we know each other well, he says I always feel and taste like something new.

"You and me. Now and forever," he murmurs between kisses. I pull away to look at him. Did he just say forever?

"What are you talking about?" I ask. He smiles his signature boyish, slightly sheepish smile.

"You asked me what I dreamt about. And now you know – I will always dream of you, Layla."

I should be used to it by now, but Noah has surprised me yet again. As he leans in to kiss me, I wrap my arms around him and hold on tight because I don't want to let go of this familiar feeling that suddenly feels brand new.

Book Playlist

❖ Only One – Felix Cartal & Karen Harding

o For the beginning of the book. This sets the dreamy, romantic tone while incorporating a catchy city nightlife vibe.

❖ (I Just) Died In Your Arms (Extended Remix) – Cutting Crew

o The song that's first playing in Layla's first dream.

❖ Never Gonna Give You Up – Rick Astley

o The song Layla and Noah dance to in her first dream.

❖ Take Me Home Tonight – Eddie Money

o The song Brandon plays when he's driving Layla home in her second dream.

❖ Right Here Waiting – Richard Marx

o The song for the love triangle of Brandon, Melody, and Jackson.

❖ If You Leave (From "Pretty In Pink") – Orchestral Manoeuvres In The Dark

o The song Melody and Jackson are dancing to in Layla's last dream.

❖ Pull Me Deep – Logan Henderson

o This is what Noah's experiencing as he realizes Layla has a gift. (Please note that I did not include this scene in the book. This is what happens at the end of Chapter 8 and before the beginning of Chapter 9.)

❖ No Distraction – Beck

o The song for when Noah finds Layla at the rooftop restaurant and they go for a walk.

❖ Another Life – Big Time Rush

o This is what Noah is going through at the end of Chapter 12 up until the end of Chapter 14. He's realizing what he wants in life and acting on his feelings for Layla.

❖ Somebody – Dagny

o The song that concludes Layla and Noah's story.

Don't miss out!

Visit the website below and you can sign up to receive emails whenever Genevieve Leanne Dominguez publishes a new book. There's no charge and no obligation.

https://books2read.com/r/B-A-VFUZ-JSIMF

BOOKS2READ

Connecting independent readers to independent writers.

Also by Genevieve Leanne Dominguez

The Moonlight Thrills Series
Moonlight Thrills
Starlight Adventure
Evening Dangers
Midnight Perils
The Moonlight Thrills Series: The Complete Collection

Standalone
When I Dream of You
Phoenix: A Small Poetry Collection
Knight: A Small Poetry Collection
Meryle and Lancelot's Adventures

Watch for more at https://genevieveleanne.wixsite.com/
mysite.

About the Author

Genevieve Leanne Dominguez, born and raised in Texas, now lives on the East Coast. She earned a B.A. in English from the University of Central Florida in 2020.

Writing, editing, and self-publishing her books is her primary hobby. Her goal is to entertain readers or help readers learn something positive. She would love to do that for many readers, but if she could do that for just one reader, then she will have done what she has set out to do as an indie author.

She likes playing video games and finding new music. She loves the autumn season and her favorite days are cloudy, rainy days. Werewolves and phoenixes are her favorite mythical creatures.

Visit her website to contact her.

Read more at https://genevieveleanne.wixsite.com/mysite.